MW01514637

# THE STINES III: BATTLE OF TEVEAHNA

# THE
# STINES IIII
## BATTLE OF TEVEAHNA

James D. Lee

**PALMETTO**
PUBLISHING

Charleston, SC
www.PalmettoPublishing.com

*The Stines III*
Copyright © 2022 by James D. Lee

The Stines III: Battle of Teveahna is a work of Fiction. Names, places, and incidents either are products of the author's imagination or are used fictitiously.

All rights reserved

No part of this book may be reproduced, stored in a retrieval system, or transmitted in any form or by any means without the prior written permission of the publishers, except by a reviewer who may quote brief passages in a review to be printed in a newspaper, magazine, or journal.

All characters in this book are fictitious.
Any resemblance to real persons, living or dead, is coincidental.

Hardcover ISBN: 979-8-88590-719-4
Paperback ISBN: 979-8-88590-721-7
eBook ISBN: 979-8-88590-720-0

This book is dedicated to

Sir Christopher Frank Carandini Lee

Richard "Rusty" Knight

Tommie Nell Lee

Cover by James D Lee and Gabe Eltaeb

# Table of Contents

# PROLOGUE:

## The Stines

### The Stines Book 1 Recap:

Mary Jade VonStine is a young lady, age 17. Mary's life is rocked by the murders of her parents. As her world is turned upside down, she finds a mysterious note from her father, who was the District Attorney of Kerverland, Mississippi.

But in truth, he was Victor Fredrick VonStine, heir to the throne of Boldovia. The note that Victor left Mary stated to contact the family in Boldovia, and for her to go there for her safety.

The best friend of Victor is Sherriff David Phillips. When David read the note, he was shocked, but got his phone out and called the number. David was able to get a hold of someone and was able to give them all the information he hand and contact information to keep them in touch.

Several weeks would pass, and no signs of who killed Mary's Parents. With all this, a court case was called, to determine what would happen to Mary.

Overseeing the case was judge John Michael Lepedrum, an older and very wise judge. The case would be highly emotional as many of the city voiced their views on what should happen. As the case was winding down a pale tall man named Velmar Von Shuffler and two red-headed ladies came into the courthouse to represent a Baron

VonStine, who was the relatives Victor had said call. After Velmar turned over the documents to show who the Baron was and the judge reading Victor's letter, the judge ordered Mary to go to Boldovia and live with Baron VonStine, but there were conditions that the Baron would have to meet.

Mary would leave with Velmar in a cavalcade of escorted cars to take her to the airport to leave for Boldovia. But they made one stop at the Sherriff's house to get some things for Mary. After that, they were on their way to the airport. As they arrived at the airport, they would be taken to the tarmac and then to a private plane waiting for them.

As Mary was flying to Boldovia she was told the story of what happened so many years ago, and the monsters who lived in the country. The monsters were all her relatives, and that they would protect her. Mary then found out that in fact, she was the heir and not the Baron for the Baron a monster himself as her protector as was the rest of the family.

The main power of the family was the vampires Count Valdisoph Vicious VonKomFoang and his daughter Lillian Diana VonStine. Lillian was the wife of the Baron VonStine a true Monster made of Magic and Science. After those were Edward VonStine, son of the Baron and Lillian. Edward was a werewolf and pack leader of a group known as the pack. The pack was made up of Edwards girlfriend Tasha Vanderfang and her brothers. After all, these were the guards and staff of the castle.

When Mary arrived in Boldovia. She was quickly taken to the old capital Teveahna. Here she was meet by Lillian and Edward and the pack, along with everyone from the city. After meeting with the people of the city she was quickly taken to the VonStine manor house to meet the family and things did not go as planned by the Count and Baron, they were stunned by how much Mary knew of the family and how strong-willed she was.

By morning it was all out in the world, the heir to the throne of Boldovia was in the castle, and home. It was a shock back in Kerverland that no one ever knew about Mary or to the fact Victor had always been the heir to the throne. Mary would make her mark quickly by making public appearances and then acting to repair her city and help her people.

The more Mary did, she hoped to lure out her parent's killers to come to get her. Mary would keep this rolling to the point of rebuilding almost all of downtown.

Mary would have to attend school in which she would meet a young man named Albert Ludwig, and basically, they would become an item after a while. Mary and Albert who at the time looked like a grunge rocker, were always together as Mary worked on her city master plan.

After a while, thanks to Mary would give Albert a total makeover, and what a makeover he turned out to be a handsome hunk of a young man.

While all this was going down Mary would find out the truth about who she was and who her mother was. Mary was the daughter of a lady named Isis VonStine. Isis in truth was the daughter of the Egyptian Cat-Goddess Bastet, Which made Mary the granddaughter of the Egyptian gods. Anubis Sek-met, and Bastet. She would learn as she would sleep of the history of her mother and what she could do, which continues to this day.

Once Mary Graduated from high school and turned eighteen, Mary made it clear Albert was her boyfriend and she was not going to hear anything about it. Even though everyone had accepted Albert from the start.

Mary would have to go to the new capital, to be made the Princess of Boldovia and get all the power that was rightfully hers. As Mary arrived in parliament, she would give a speech that would rock the nation. Calling out the murders of her parents and then take her government to task for not taking care of her people instead of putting personal gains first.

Mary would lay out a full plan to fix her countries problems and even pay for it and would catch everyone in the government off guard and embarrassed as she finished, she did not call for any resignations, but she put her government on notice.

After all, this going down, Mary had things in motion and now waited for the murders to come for her, and her family would be ready. It would not take long for the murders would now know about Mary and the leaders a Sir Walter Lee and Johnathon Thomas of the VH corporation a front for a monster-hunting operation.

After the monster hunters had their plans done and ready to move out. Albert had hacked all their systems and watched everything now the Count and the rest were ready, and the war was going to start soon.

It was not long, and they came in using stealth helicopters. There were six four-man teams, and they would break up into three sets of two teams each. One group would come in from the base of the mountain and the second group would come in at the manor house, and the last two teams would attack the Castle.

The battle started with the two teams at the base of the mountain. Heading up towards the manor house, they would be attacked by Edward and the full power of the pack of werewolves. This battle would have to be hit and run and, in the end, half of the pack would be killed in the battle with Edward and Tasha hurt.

As the next two teams attacked the manor house, this would be a massive blood bath with the Count, and Baron taking a major part in the fight. Though Catherine, Mary's aid would die in this battle. The monster hunters would all fall with two being turned into vampires to serve the Count.

Finally, the last two teams hit the castle and the front of the castle would cause an explosion and bring down the gate and killing many of the guards, but the fire fight would take place as one team stayed to fight, and another went into the Castle. Inside the Castle, more fighting would take place as the leader of all the teams James Davidson and one other would make it into Mary's bedroom and face off against Lillian VonStine. Lillian would kill the one monster hunter and fight against James who was an augmented soldier. As James came in for the final kill on Lillian, Mary would step in and cause James to stop for Mary was the main target he was to kill. As he spoke the area changed and they all were now in the land of the gods and at that point, Sek-Met would take over. Sek-Met would totally rip into James, taking off both of his hands. Sek-met gave him no chance and would pound on him over and over breaking bone after bone. If not for being in the realm of the gods James would already be dead for sure.

While Sek-Met kept attacking James, Bastet would see to Lillian and heal her and give her a gift of protection from the rays of Ra since she was a daughter of Ra. As Lillian got up and heard James call for mercy and give out that Lillian's mother Mina was still alive. Lillian in rage would attack James till he gave the location of where Mina was, and Bastet would pull her off him. Sek-Met at that point would drag James off to inside the temple, and his final fate would be sealed.

As Mary and Lillian were now back in her room the rest of the family would arrive to make sure all was okay and battle if need be. As the city police force arrived and aided in the battle out front reports would show up. Mary would give a statement on what had happened.

It would be several days, but Mary and the family would see to their dead loved ones. This hit Mary hard with the loss of Catherine who had helped her so much. As the funeral let out Mary would make a statement. Mary said, "Morning is over now comes Vengeance and I will have my Vengeance that I promise you." With this Mary and the family would return to the castle.

# END Book 1
# The Stines

# PROLOGUE:

## The Stines II: Carmella

### The Stines Book 2 Recap:

As we continue with part two of the story, we find the VH corporation in total disarray and as Walter Lee went to his ancestral home, he would be stopped by his younger half-brother Richard Henry Lee. Richard would try and warn Walter about their grandmother acting strange, but Walter would not listen.

Walter as usual would not listen to his brother and would fall to the vampire Carmella, who was masquerading as the Lee's grandmother. Carmella would then find out what had happened and take over running the VH corporation and start to plan her war against the VonStines for she hated them all with a passion. Carmella would eventually find out the truth behind Mary VonStine and who her mother was and in turn devise a way to meet the young princess.

Meanwhile the relationships between Mary and Albert would move to the next level as Albert and Mary would get engaged along with Edward and Tasha. While all the celebration Carmella would send a letter to Mary about returning her parents heads to her. In which would lead to Mary meeting Carmella face to face.

With the outcome now having Mary involved in Carmella's war. But unknown to Carmella the count along with the family would make their way to England by way of invitation of the Queen of England.

While in England Mary along with Albert and Lily would go and meet with the queen. The queen would have a long talk with Mary and explain many things about being a ruler. After tea Mary would start to explain everything about the VH corporation to the queen and how they were monster hunters that the queens father had disbanded back in the 1940s.

While this was going on the count along with the baron and the pack would attack Cotton Hall Castle and the VH corporation. They would be joined by Tarja and her two brothers and later by Richard Henry Lee the younger half-brother of Walter Lee and Tarja boyfriend. With the battle going on the castle would be turned upside down in looking for Mina but she along with Walter would be long gone. It would take a while before Richard could figure out where his brother had run off to.

Back at the palace the queen had called for the prime minister and the top men of MI-6 for a meeting which Mr. Thomas the mastermind behind the hunters was part of. When they arrived, Mr. Thomas was shocked to see Mary and the rest there but keep his cool for now. The queen would demand an explanation of what was going on and throw the folder with evidence at the men. The prime minster nor the head of MI-6 could explain any of what they were looking at.

While all the events played out in the palace under the city of London the count and his people would eventually find Walter Lee and Carmella. But at first not recognize Carmella do to she was disguised, and in the end, Carmella would kill Walter Lee and almost kill her own sister Mina. But at the last minute the count and his people would save Mina and Carmella would escape to fight another day. Though one of Tarja's brothers would fall in battle during the fighting in the underground.

After saving Mina the whole party would race up into the palace just in time to be there when Mary would send everyone including the queen and the prime minster, the head of MI-6 and Mr. Thomas into the den realm. Which all would face Bastet, Sek-met at first and finally Anubis himself.

Anubis would judge Mr. Thomas and pass judgement on him, for all the evil he had done and had to pay for his sin's.

The queen along with Mary and Albert along with the prime minster would make a public announcement of what took place and close the chapter on Mary's parents murders. Finally, there was closer in Mary's parents deaths and now Mary could look to the Future with Albert and the rest of her family.

Several months would pass but finally Mary would be crowned Queen of Boldovia, and everyone attended even several of the gods.

Edward and Tasha would get married and as a present Mary had VonStine keep at the lake updated and remodeled as a wedding gift for them. Which they gladly excepted. While the remodel was going on the workers would find a side tunnel from the main tunnel that connected the keep with the VonStine castle and VonStine manor. This tunnel would lead to the missing VonStine treasure vault and inside the massive Dragon Night Star who guarded it would be found.

Mary and Night Star would become friends and she would visit the Dragon often to learn what he had seen firsthand in all his years alive. Mary would learn of the secret passage that lead to the lake and how the Dragon had always keep out of sight even as big as he was.

Mary would also learn of her own powers as she was able to produce claws out of her fingernails which shocked everyone. In the end Mary and Albert would actually train with Bastet and Sek-met in how to fight and use her powers now that she was mature.

While this training was going on Horus would arrive and take over training with Albert and finally the gods would work with both of them as a team giving them armor and Albert a set of swords so that he could fight alongside Mary. This training would go on for several months until they were able to really fight together as a team.

Finally, the day came for Mary and Albert to get married and what a wedding it was as the whole country turned out for it. Mary would be in a magnificent white dress and Albert would be in his dress military uniform. The wedding was a thing for the ages as it was so magical.

# 1

# Carmella's Story

I507 Duke Valmor's Castle was fixing to be under attack from the Turkish Army and he had been ordered to leave and go to the VonStine Castle for protection. But in his arrogance the Duke had refused which was unbeknown to Carmella Valmor the older sister of Mina VonKomfoang the wife of Count VonKomfoang. For this would turn to be a fatal mistake costing the Duke his life and destruction of Castle Valmor. As Duke Valmor would fall protecting his daughter but Carmella would suffer at the hands of the Turkish army and be raped for days on end. In her mind the VonStines had abandoned her and her father and betrayed them in her mind. She wanted revenge on the VonStines and especially her sister Mina.

Finally, after days of hell, Carmella escaped her captives, but her body was scared with whip lashes and all of the soldiers using her as they wanted. Her long golden hair had been cut off and her body was bruised and battered. As Carmella wandered the lands she came upon a cave and stumbled into it crying she cried for vengeance and revenge. Carmella wanted that more than anything and cursed everyone and everything. As Carmella was doing this, she heard a noise coming from deep inside the cave and could smell smoke and felt fire as she went deeper into the cavern. There Carmella saw a fire burning and by it a black coffin. The lid of the coffin was off and, in a chair, sat a man in all black robes. His eyes were red as fire and before Carmella could say a word the man was up out of the chair and across the room with his hand on Carmella's Throat.

The man opened his mouth showing the Vampiric fangs and was fixing to bite Carmella but stopped as he sensed as though Carmella did not care and her heart was stone cold. The man dropped Carmella to the ground and walked back to his chair.

"You are very interesting you are already cold in the heart like me but are still human. Who are you and why are you like that?" The vampire said. Carmella sat on the floor and looked at the vampire." I was Carmella Diana Valmor oldest daughter of the Duke Valmor." Carmella replied. "I don't care what you are or what you do to me all I want is revenge of my sister and her husband Count Valdisoph Vicious VonKomfoang who betrayed my father and me and left us to the Turks who killed my father and did this to me." Carmella screamed in anger.

The man smiled his fangs showing again. "I was once , Prince Vadisloff Von Dracu Tempest of Transylvania but now I am just Dracu. Your Count Valdisoph Vicious VonKomFoang and I have crossed past just a few years past. Before I was betrayed and cursed to become a Vampire. But you, I can sense you would ravish this power I have, and you would use it for your revenge." Dracu said. At which Carmella looked at the one in black robes with interest. "I will make you a deal my Carmella. I will make you a Vampire like myself with all the powers that come with it. But you will be mine for all times. My bride you could say. Do we have a deal? "the prince asked seeing if Carmella would take the offer or not.

Carmella smiled devilishly and without a second thought said "Yes" to the offer and without a second to reconsider the prince had her in his arms and his fangs sank deep into her neck. When Carmella awoke, she was beautiful again with her long blond hair now immortal and always beautiful she turned and looked at her new master and smiled. "Oh, I am going to enjoy this my master" she said in a wicked tone.

"Good, Good now we must rest come my bride and when you awaken you may turn the world red with blood." The prince said to Carmella.

Carmella sleep peacefully for the first time in a long time and she dreamed of her revenge and how she was going to paint VonStine castle in blood. When Carmella and Dracu awoke Carmella found herself not in the cave but in a catacomb of some type of building. Dracu got out of the coffin and helped Carmella get out. Carmella felt amazing and as she looked around, she would look at herself in a mirror and see her body was so beautiful again as well as her face was perfect with her long blond hair. Carmella turned and looked at Dracu and smiled at him. "This is amazing I never thought I would ever be like this. Thank you, Master," Carmella said with some happiness in her voice.

Dracu smiled and clapped his hands for an assistant to come to them. An older man came in and bowed to both Dracu and Carmella "you summoned master" the man said.

"Yes, Marcus find my bride Carmella some elegant dresses" Dracu said.

"Any color in particular my lady?" Marcus asked.

Carmella smiled and said "Yes red, I love red." Marcus bowed and then left the area.

Once Carmella was dressed in a lovely red dress, Dracu would give her a tour of his castle which was on the other side of the mountain that the cave Carmella had found Dracu in.

As the tour ran down and Dracu and Carmella walked into the throne room of the Castle Dracu stopped and Carmella looked at the Throne. Sitting on the Throne was a Cat but not any ordinary cat but the black cat with white paws. The cat licked its paw and then looked at both Dracu and Carmella. "Greetings Prince Dracu and you as well Duchess Carmella Valmor" was herd in their heads.

Carmella looked around not fully understanding until Dracu finally said something. "Well, this is an unexpected visit. What do we owe your presence today little one?" Dracu asked.

Once again, the voice was herd "Oh great prince I am here not to berate you in any ways but give a message to your new bride Carmella." Carmella was shocked and looked at the cat.

"Oh, and what message do you have for my bride" Dracu asked.

"To you Carmella you wish war on the VonStine's but know this your war will be contained to Boldovia and the area around that country unless a part of the other side is outside that realm and starts fighting. You are strictly forbidden from actions outside that area. For the great prince is no more and his son now rules as has the Count fallen and become as you both are. Know this is a war between the families and it is to be keep that way. For that is the words of the Master. "The voice said.

Dracu was shocked "Wait VonKomfoang has fallen and become like myself?" Dracu asked. The cat only nodded its head. Carmella also was shocked but smiled in seeing her vengeance was already taken place somewhat and she would have plenty of time to get her vengeance. "And If I break these rules then what. "Carmella said spitefully. At which point Carmella found herself standing in sand in front of the temple of Karnak and sitting in front of her was the gods Bastet, Sek-Met and Anubis.

Anubis looked at Carmella "if you break my rules Carmella, I will Judge you just like I do all Vampires. You have power but with power comes with rules and you best follow those rules. I judge all equally and without malice." Anubis said in his dark deep voice.

With that everything was back to normal, and the cat had vanished. Dracu looked to Carmella. "remember what you have seen for Anubis is over all of us that are undead." Dracu stated to Carmella. Carmella was not happy with this turn of events but none the less she had all the time in the world to bring hell on earth to the VonStines and Boldovia.

# 2

# Liechtenstein

The Royal Train had just crossed the boarders of Boldovia and Liechtenstein and was just about thirty minutes out from the capital city of Vaduz. The capital city was not very large maybe about one-tenth the size of Teveahna. As the train pulled into the station at Schaan it was greeted by an official delegation from the Prince of Liechtenstein. The actual Capital of Vaduz has no airport or train station but is only about maybe one kilometer away from Schaan.

As the party from Boldovia came out of the small train station several cars were waiting on them so they could travel the short distance to the capital city.

As the cars left the train station their host who was a servant of the Prince of Liechtenstein gave Mary and her party a short version of the history of the country and of what the main imports and exports were of the country. Mary was paying close attention to what the man was saying. She needed to learn all she could so she could turn things around in her country and make it as prominent as both Liechtenstein and Switzerland.

The cars arrived at a small hotel in the Capital. It was a classic hotel, like a four-story lodge for skiing but still very nice. Albert was first to get out along with Edward and then came Mary and Tasha. Behind them in the next three cars was the rest of the party. They had the whole hotel to themselves and made sure to give extra to the owners for their stay.

As they checked in to the hotel they were showing to the rooms for the night. Mary and Albert had a dinner engagement with the Prince later in the day. So, for now, it was downtime to rest and just enjoy the time in the country.

Meanwhile deep in the Carpathian Mountains, high up on top of a mountain sat the ruins of the keep of Valdivian in which it was said that evil dwelt in the mountain for it once was a mountain of fire that had long since slept.

As the sun was setting Carmella arrived and went into the ruins for, she knew this place very well for it was the one place she felt safe and could relax. As she went further into the ruins and down into the tunnels of the mountain, she found many warriors training in some of the open caverns in the mountain. A smile came over her face, which was very rare. Carmella finally came into a hall unlike all the others it was lite better than the rest and the walls were very regal in the design along with red carpet on the floor going to two large doors engraved with a dragon taking up both doors. Carmella stopped at the doors and slipped out of her clothing handing her dress to a servant and leaving her boots to the side.

The Guards at the door opened them and bowed to the now nude Carmella as she passed by them. Her body was pale without any marks she was amazingly beautiful with her long blond hair handing down her back. As she came into the room it was covered in a red carpet with a fireplace on one wall. Near the center was a regal throne of gold and cider with red cushions. Sitting on this throne was a man that looked to be in his early forties with long black hair that went just past his shoulders. He was dressed in all Black as his handheld a book open as if he was reading it.

The man in black looked up seeing Carmella and smiled at her. "Ah my lovely bride you have returned," the man in black said in a loving voice. Carmella bowed to the man in black "Greetings my beloved Master it is good to see you" Carmella replied. The man in black put his book away and patted his lap. "Come sit with me and let me enjoy your company." The man in black commanded. Carmella smiled and walked over and sat on the man in black's lap and as she did, she tilted her head slightly to the side offering her neck to the man in black. The man in black did not wait long as his fangs sank into Carmella's neck.

Carmella let out a soft moan for to her it was very pleasurable almost erotic in feeling for her. For this was not just a Vampire for this was Carmella's master in who she owned everything, and he was the one who saved her and gave her a new lease on life. Carmella loved the man in black for he was the only one back in the day to take her in and truly made her a princess of this prince.

"Mmm... you always taste so sweet my bride," The man in black said as he pulled his fangs from Carmella's neck. Carmella gave her master a passionate kiss and smiled at him. His hands rested on Carmella's nude body. "I have missed you, my master. But alas I had to set things in motion for my revenge as you promised me long ago. "Carmella said in a sweet tone. "yes, yes, I remember the promise I made to you But tell me what of this new Queen and your plans. I am so enjoying watching all this play out. But a word of caution bride you are like a moth to the flame, and you may not survive you move to fast. "The man in black said.

"Of course, beloved but now I must ask you for the army you built for me. All is set the Queen is out of the country on her honeymoon and the people are too focused on partying to see an attack coming. Especially my brother-in-law the Count." Carmella said leaning into a hug the man in black gave her. "Are you sure my bride for you only get one chance at this and if you fail you will not be coming home ever again." The man in black said to her. "Yes, beloved it is time, for now, those in Egypt cannot protect the queen or her people. I have already placed some men in places so that when I move the country will be shut down and it will be weeks before anyone can come to save the VonStines and in the end, they will die, and I will kill the queen and then vanish to return and be at your side for all times." Carmella said explaining what she was going to do. The man in black just smiled. Carmella would stay the rest of the night with her master to show him her thanks and love.

Meanwhile back in Liechtenstein Albert and Mary were enjoying a very elegant dinner with the crowned prince and his wife. Mary had been seeking advice on how to turn her economy around and make it as prosperous as Liechtenstein was. The prince explained how he along with his parliament had set up a strong financial sector for those who needed a place to put money and not face super high taxes or backlash for being rich. In return, these people would invest in the local businesses and economy to grow it and make it stronger. Mary understood a tax haven for those who were rich in return they would invest and help the local economy to grow strong and make the country self-sufficient in away.

The rest of the dinner would be more on how Mary was handling being Queen and how she was dealing with ruling her country sense she and the prince of Liechtenstein were the only two rulers who still had control of their countries. Mary was surprised by that but was learning much from the prince and she would take what she learned back home after her honeymoon.

After dinner, Mary and Albert returned to the hotel to relax as much as a newlywed couple would always.

While Mary and Albert were at dinner, Edward and Tasha were out enjoying the night walking down the streets and stopping in a couple of sidewalk cafes. It was really the first time they had ever been away from the capital in their lives, and they were out seeing everything. "You know if you would have told me we would be here married enjoying the night outside of just the old capital I would have said it would be a wonderful dream but never happen." Tasha said to Edward as she snuggled up to him as they walked. Edward smiled and wrapped his arm around Tasha "Oh I know, mom and dad always talked about the prince coming home, and then when it was Mary and not her father. That first night when she came out in that red sweater and mom pulled her hood down and she stood there. I was like this is a dream, and the dream never ended, and it's been better than I could have ever dreamed of even grandmother is back as well." Edward said as they keep walking.

"Yes, I remember that night as well and then school and Albert. I mean Albert who would have seen that coming. Look at him now Prince Albert married to Mary and looking like he does now. No one saw that coming at all." Tasha replied. Edward laughed thinking about all of it. "Yes, so true it's all a dream and one I do not want to wake up from ever." Edward said and then kissed Tasha as they walked.

As the moon was out and bright John and Rebecca sat enjoying some warm tea as they sat just outside the hotel letting the young couples have some time to themselves. John was always one to keep an eye out for trouble and had promised the count that he would always keep everyone safe. The pack was out in about keeping an eye on Edward and Tasha but also giving them space. Rebecca looked over at John." You seemed troubled little brother" Rebecca said. John smiled "No just thinking is all." John replied. "Oh really, let me guess. Your thinking of what you and father are going to talk about. Or you going to soon be a great grandfather and then have to deal with all those little ones running around that castle." Rebecca said jokingly.

John laughed "no little children in the castle would be a blessing for everyone especially for the count and baron and the ladies. They would be all over them and pampering them. I am thinking of father for he and I are still not on great terms, and I wonder what is so important that he requested all of us to come to Monaco." John said to his sister.

Rebecca sighed "John I really don't know what father wants he would not even tell me. But it has to be serious that is for sure. He has been on edge even calling all of his warriors to the training area's out in the mountains near Monaco." Rebecca said. This got John very concerned as he looked to his sister. "Wait he called in all the warriors; father has never done that before something is definitely wrong. But do me a favor don't tell the youngsters let them enjoy the honeymoon let's just keep all this to you and me. Till we know what is going on." John told his sister.

Rebecca smiled and nodded in agreement with her brother's suggestion. "Alright till then we will let them enjoy the honeymoon," Rebecca replied.

The rest of the night was peaceful and enjoyable for the newly-wed couples and when morning came the pack and John along with Rebecca were already in the lobby when the young couples came down to join them. John would go over the days' plans as they would be leaving on the train in a few hours to head on to Monaco and then they could enjoy the vacation and honeymoon. Everyone was excited and was ready to go.

It would be 10 am when the train was ready to load. Mary, Albert, Edward, and Tasha would be in the back-privet car while the pack along with John and Rebecca would be in the next car. The Train would pull away from the station and head on its way to Monaco. It would be an all-day trip through the mountains, but no one minded the time or the trip as the landside was so beautiful with mountains and waterfalls as they went thought the mountains.

As the train headed to Monaco, Carmella had returned to her castle ruins and this time she had her army with her. There Greggor was waiting as his brother Demitriof was already in Monaco waiting for the Queen and her party to arrive. All was set as Carmella came into the ruins and hugged her son. "I take it Demitriof is in Monaco already," Carmella said. Greggor nodded "Yes mother all is set up he and his men will attack the Wolf Kings court when we attack the city and VonStine mountain." Carmella smiled wickedly at her son. "Very good, very good indeed, have the men move out I want a blitz attack to cut off the old capital from everyone the weather will be bad so no air attack can take place. And your men inside the new join base will make sure all the aircraft will be inoperable. "Carmella asked her son. Greggor nodded "yes mother all is set to go we should be able to attack within a day or two and when we go it will be fast and we will have everyone.

In the city of Teveahna, the train from the capital arrived and Jay Lester Morgan stepped off the train and looked around as he walked out of the station. Morgan thought to himself that the city really had changed since the last time he was here. Morgan walked out into the square and a car pulled up. The back door opened, and a voice called to Morgan. "Get in," a female voice said. Morgan looked inside and was surprised to see Sek-Met there.

"Well don't just stand there get in," Sek-Met said again. Morgan put his bags in the trunk and got in the car. "Well, this is a surprise so what news do you have for me," Morgan asked. "Carmella is moving up her attack you will have to get as many of Mary's guards out of the castle before she attacks it. If you don't, they will all be killed." Sek-Met explained to Morgan. "And the Count and the rest ?" Morgan asked.

"You will have to let them be. Mary will need you and her guards. Inside the castle is an elevator that leads down to the catacombs use that to get to the tunnels that take you to VonStine keep. Once there wait for Mary to show up and then plan your counterattack. But do not face off with Carmella and her army till Mary gets here with reinforcements." Sek-Met ordered.

"So, it's going to be a war in the city between the two armies. This should be fun. Just remember our agreement on that clean slate." Morgan said. Sek-Met just smiled as Morgan was dropped off at a safe house to get ready for combat.

# 3

# Arrive in Monaco

After three days of traveling the royal train finally arrived in the city state of Monaco. The royal train pulled into the Monte Carlo Station early in the morning. The station sits on the boarders of Monaco and France and is in walking distance to almost everything in the city state.

As Mary and the rest of her group came off the train they were meet by representatives of both Monaco and France. After the normal formalities were done. Mary and the group were taken to their hotel which was the Novotel Monte Carlo Hotel. Which was right down in the middle of the city.

Mary and her group checked in at the hotel and were shown to the top floor. The whole floor was going to be theirs. The rooms were massive, and Mary and Albert's room had an amazing view of the sea. Once Mary and Albert were all settled in a representative of the Prince of Monaco arrived to go over some official things.

"Greetings your Majesty and welcome to Monte Carlo it is a pleasure for us to have you here and congratulations on your marriage and hope you enjoy your honeymoon while here. "The Princes representative said. "I am Sir De Val and will be your liaison while you are here." Sir De Val stated.

Mary smiled "Thank you Sir De Val and we are so far having a wonderful time in Monaco. "Mary said.

De Val nodded "Very good so let me go over these things with you. Tomorrow the formula one racers will be open for fans to meet and of course you and your group will get a tour. Then the afternoon is all yours to enjoy. Followed by tomorrow night's formal dinner with the Prince and his family. Then the day after is of course the formula one race and we have it set for you and your husband to join His Majesty for the race. If that is alright with you. "De Val said.

Mary and Albert both smiled. "Of course, that would be great may I bring my Cousin and his wife who is with us to the race as well." Mary asked.

De Val nodded. "Of course, I will see to the arrangements and will meet everyone tomorrow morning. If there is nothing else, I will take my leave." De Val stated.

Mary looked to Albert and then back to De Val. "Till tomorrow then Sir De Val." Mary said.

With that De Val bowed and turned and left the room. As De Val walked down the hall to the elevator, he called the Prince's office and made arrangements. As the Elevator opened De Val was shocked to see John and Rebecca and stopped in his tracks.

As Rebecca looked at Del Val. De Val Bowed to both of them. "Greetings Lady Rebecca and Sir John, it is good to see you both again.

John nodded to De Val "Good to see you De Val it's been years, but you have not changed at all." John said.

De Val nodded and took out a note and gave it to John. "It's from your father he said to give it to you when I crossed your path." De Val said.

John took the letter and opened it. Rebecca looked over Johns shoulder to see what the letter said.

"Hello John.
I hope you and the family are well, I am.
Writing you to inform you that it seems Carmella.
has started to move and I believe she may try a
Attack on your party. Also, I wish to speak with

you and your Queen after the race.
King Zagreus III"

John read the letter as did Rebecca who had a smile on her face for the moment. "I will let the Queen know and we will meet with my Father. So, let him know De Val we will meet after the race." John said.

De Val nodded and smiled. "Of course, Sir John. I will let the king know and I am sure he will be happy to see you. "De Val said. With that De Val stepped into the elevator and let the doors closed. John and Rebecca talked for a moment.

"It was nice seeing father and the count get along for once." John said to Rebecca.

"Yes, It was something and now father is very happy seeing Tasha and Edward married as well. The family line still grows as it should. But remember big brother father has not totally forgiving you for leaving us for the count. So, walk lightly around him for a start. But I think father has taken a liking to the Queen of yours. She is something special that's for sure." Rebecca told John.

John nodded he knew all too well how his father felt about him and his choice to be with the count after the war. John still remembered the heated argument that happened and how his father had almost disowned him for his choice. But now maybe just maybe things could return to the way they had been before the war. For now, John would just have to wait and see. His job was to keep Mary safe on her honeymoon and that was what he was going to do.

Mary and Albert relaxed on the patio and looked out over the city and out to the sea and it was just magical. Mary leaned over and kissed Albert and smiled. "Well, it's our honeymoon and we can just relax tonight," Mary said.

Albert smiled and nodded "Yes, it's already a magical time, I would never have thought any of this would happen it's been so wonderful to be with you and I could not see being with you ever." Albert said.

While Mary and Albert were relaxing in their room Edward and Tasha had stepped out and started to walk around the city. They were also on their honeymoon and were out enjoying the night. After all Monte Carlo is the hidden kingdom of the Werewolves and Tasha was the Kings great granddaughter. It was strange as they walked the streets some people stopped and bowed to Tasha in respect, they knew who she was, and it was the first time to be in the city in person but her wedding photo with Edward had made it through out the kingdom.

Tasha had her arm around Edwards and was right up next to him as they walked down Boulevard du Larvotto. Tasha saw the Rossi Ice Cream shop and nugged Edward. Edward smiled and they stopped and got some Ice cream and then keep walking on down to the sea to sit and enjoy the night.

While the night was turning into a romantic night for both couples another train had arrived in Monti Carlo. As the door of the last car opened up a large man with black hair came off this was none other than Demitriof Valmor the younger son of Carmella and yes, he was a vampire, and he was here on business. Demitriof was meet by two men in black suits and the three of them went and got into a black Jaguar and left for a privet home.

As the Jaguar pulled inside the house's garage the three men got out and went into the main living room. There Demitriof was meet by five other men. "Report now." Demitriof said.

One man bowed "Greetings Lord Demitriof, we have both couples being shadowed at moment the Queen and her husband are in the hotel" The man said point at the map. "The Werewolf couple are on the beach at moment. And the rest are in the hotel resting." The man finished saying.

Demitriof nodded liking what he herd. "Good, and how many men are here for the attack on the Kings lair," He asked.

"We have two hundred and fifty ghouls ready and waiting to attack. We will hit them from three sides, and we have learned that the king has requested a meeting with Queen Mary and her group the night after the race. So, everyone will be in one place, and we can hit them and destroy all of them in one attack. It will stay inside the Wolves Lair and not spill out into the city." The man said as he explained things to Demitriof.

Demitriof was very pleased. "Good mother will be pleased. Once we take the Queens head the main army will attack the Stines Castle and Manor house and then the city will fall to us. We will have our vengeance against the Stines at last. The country of Boldovia will fall and the world will see the truth the country has hidden for over five hundred years." Demitriof said as he went in and saw the little girl chained in the bedroom.

He closed the door and feed on the girl for he had not had any blood for two days. Demitriof looked over the map of the Wolves Lair more and more wanting to make sure all was perfect for the attack. He smiled devilishly as he could see all the people dead in his mind.

# 4

# Albert, Mary, Edward, Tasha Honeymoon

As the sun came up Albert and Mary woke up and got out of bed and dressed for the day. They were to be escorted with everyone down to meet the drivers and crews of the formula one race. Which Mary and Edward and many of the pack wanted to really do. For they all loved cars and they wanted to really get a good look at the state-of-the-art race cars.

As everyone meet in the dining hall for breakfast Sir De Val arrived to meet everyone. With De Val was Rebecca and her three children two boys and a girl. The three were close to the pack and the rest age. After everyone was introduced and had breakfast, the group would leave with De Val and head to where the race cars were garaged.

The day was warm and sunny as they got to the garages they were meet by security and then was escorted on in. Mary and Edward were like kids in a candy store talking with the owners and mechanics. The mechanics went through how the specialized breaking systems worked and how the hybrid engines worked in general terms not giving away the real secrets to the cars themselves.

Mary and Edward keep talking about the cars and what could be done with the integra and the rat rods to make the suspension even better than what they had on the cars. John looked at Albert and

Tasha and just shook his head. "Yes, we all knew this was going to happen. Hopefully, it will get out of their system by lunch." John said.

Albert was not so sure after all once Mary had her mind made up there was no stopping her. But alas after they got though with meeting everyone and walking around some of the track it was time for the racers to do the time trials. So, Mary and the rest got to the stands and got to watch it live. Mary loved every moment of it.

But as this was going on many things were being played out in the shadows. Not only was the press taking photos of all the group, but they really were taking photos of Albert and Mary the press just could not get enough of the beautiful young queen and her handsome husband.

As the group moved around and meet with every team they were then showed where they would be watching the race from. The box seats were set up for the main straightaway of the race and the view was amazing. Mary was really looking forward to the race as was Edward.

After everything was done with what was going to happen tomorrow with the race and all. The group finally got the afternoon to enjoy and so they returned to the hotel to change and head to the beach. Of course, this was a circus as every photographer was out to get photos of the four of them and of course Mary and Tasha in their bikini swimsuits. But the members of the pack made sure to keep the press at a distance while the two couples enjoyed their honeymoon.

For a few hours, the two couples would stay on the beach, but they knew that they had a dinner date for the evening and had to get ready for it. So, when it was time, they all headed back to the hotel to get ready for the dinner.

Meanwhile back in Boldovia, Morgan was walking around the old capital city Teveahna, he noticed a lot of young men all in teams of two. This to Morgan was a red flag but to the normal person you would not think twice about it. Morgan would walk the square and take count. What he was seeing concerned him greatly for just in the square he counted sixty men.

Morgan figured to case the area's around the major buildings and the hotel. To his thinking he was right to check he found at least one hundred more men. To Morgan this was becoming not just some men that Carmella had put together but an army and one that was getting bigger as he keep walking around. But one question bothered Morgan all these men had to be ghouls and not full vampires for how else could they be out in the sun.

Morgan was starting to put it all together on how the men were laid out and how they were moving around. They like himself were casing the city, and Morgan could tell that a much larger group of men were on the east side of town closest to the manor house and castle. Morgan was thinking that when the attack hit the city the large force he had found would go after the manor house and the castle.

Morgan had to figure a way to get to the castle and get everyone out. As Morgan keep walking around, he remembered what Sek-Met told him about the tunnels under the castle that lead to the VonStine keep out near the lake. He also knew he had the letter that showed him as the queens first knight. So, Morgan finally was getting a plan put together and how he would pull off a rescue before the attack could get going.

But as Morgan was walking around, he came to a stop as he saw three people he was not expecting. Almost right in front of him coming out of a shop was Sherriff Phillips, his wife Crystal, and Judge Lepedrum. This was bad Morgan knew how close the three of those people were to the queen and he now had to come up with a way to get them to safety as well.

Just then the silver Rolls Royce pulled up and the Sherriff, his wife and the judge all got in. Morgan watched seeing the Rolls leave and head up the mountain to the castle. Morgan sighed a little in relief that those three were at the castle and would make it much easier to save everyone before the coming attack. For now, Morgan went and returned to the safe house that was provided for him.

As Morgan walked in her heard a voice. "So, I take it you scoped the whole city out." Morgan looked down and saw the black cat with white paws.

"oh, it's you" Morgan said as he walked past the cat and went into the kitchen to get something to drink. The cat followed Morgan into the kitchen. As Morgan got his beer and turned around to look at the cat, he just shook his head at the cat.

"You seem calm for what is around town and fixing to happen." The cat said. Morgan took a drink and looked at the cat.

"Not much to panic about at moment so best to stay calm. I am putting a plan together to get everyone out of the castle as soon as I can. My guess is they are waiting till most likely tomorrow night to strike. The weather in Monti Carlo will be nice but here its forecasted for rain and overcast. So, no air power can be used for at least three days. With that I will move tomorrow during the day to get to the castle and get everyone to the lake keep. That way we have a base to operate from for the mean time." Morgan explained to the cat.

The cat sat there licking its paw and then looked up at Morgan, "Interesting plan, mistress will be pleased but remember you may only be able to save the castle. So, make sure to save the humans that should be your priority." The cat said. Morgan nodded as he drank his beer. Then Morgan walked over and sat down in a chair and looked out the window as he watched what was going on outside. He knew that for now he had to wait but he was ready to act and would move out tomorrow morning.

Morgan looked over some information on the castle that he was given by Sek-met and noticed some interesting things. He saw that inside the garage was a massive fuel reserve which to him would come in handy. But he also knew it would be harder to do solo as he was now than with his old team he once had.

Morgan just sipped his beer as he looked over the photos of the mountain and what could be done to deal with a massive attack. Every once in a while Morgan would look up and out of the window. Morgan keep seeing more men and knew tomorrow would be the day he would have to fight, and he would have to win. It was all or nothing now and Morgan was in a way a dead man walking which at this moment made him the most deadly man in all of Boldovia.

Meanwhile back in Monti Carlo, Albert and Mary had gotten ready to go have dinner with the prince and his wife. "The limo had pulled up in front of the hotel as Albert and Mary came out. There was a lot of photographers out to get photos of the young queen and her husband. Albert and Mary got into the limo, and it pulled away from the hotel. It would move down to the street to the home of the prince of Monti Carlo. Albert would get out first and then help Mary out. Albert was in a black tuxedo and Mary was in a lovely white dress with lace sleaves.

As Albert and Mary entered the residence they were meet by the Prince and his wife and after a few moments they would move to the dining hall of the residence and would be seated at a table by the staff.

The dinner was a very intimate affair with just the four of them in the hall. Mary and the Prince would talk about the history of Monti Carlo and how it was able to stay an independent city state and how the state build its wealth to aid its people. This again was what Mary needed to help build up her country and bring it to be more in line with Monti Carlo and Liechtenstein. The dinner would go very well for both Mary and the Prince as they talked about a lot of things. After the dinner the Prince would go over how things would go tomorrow with the race and hoped Mary and her party would enjoy it.

# 5

# The Race and Prince
# of Monaco

The sun was up as everyone was up and about today was the day of
the race and Albert and Mary were to be with the Prince and his
wife for the race. Edward and Tasha had great seats near Albert and
Mary but before they all were seated, they were all to meet to go over
things to take place during the race.

At the privet area for celebrities the Prince and his wife welcomed
Albert and Mary and then the Prince finally saw Edward and Tasha
and the Prince was very happy to see them. "Ah Princess Tasha it is
such a wonderful moment to meet you, I hope you were able to meet
with your great grandfather for I know he is looking forward to see
you." The prince said.

Tasha smiled "No not yet we are to meet tonight with grandfather
and aunt Rebecca." Tasha said.

Mary looked at Tasha "Princess you never said anything about
that" Mary said.

The Prince laughed "Oh you did not know her great grandfather is
a king of the boarder city." The Prince replied.

Mary just smiled. With that they were lead over to the seating area
and they all got seated just as the race cars passed on the warmup lap.

As the race started and the cars took off down the city streets John
was meeting with Rebecca and his brother Marcus to discuss Mary's

meeting with their father the king of the werewolves. "Ah what it's like to be young again. The youngsters seem to be enjoying the race". Rebecca said.

John smiled "Yes, they seem to be its still so unreal to see Tasha married to Edward and of course Mary, let's face it two years ago no one even knew her and now the queen of the country and she has turned the whole country around" John said with some pride in his voice.

Travis just laughed "You have not changed at all baby brother, Still on the cloud of yours but you should be. I mean you have four great children and twelve grandchildren though we still mourn the loss of four of them. They were truly warriors of the clans for sure." Travis said with some sadness in his voice.

John looked down for a second and then to his brother. "Thank you, Travis, it really meet a lot to all of use and when father came for the wedding it just made the world to Tasha." John said.

"Father wants to see you tonight it seems he is upset and has some news on the actions of Carmella, and he is not liking it. He made it clear it was the utmost important. So, when you come Travis will be waiting for us and I will be escorting you with my four children." Rebecca said.

John knew this meeting was going to be important and he needed all that information on Carmella. John, Rebecca, and Travis finally got to sit down and enjoy the race. As the race was going the media was showing the race on television and the cameras keep panning over to get a shot of Mary. Mary was very popular in Europe. Mary was the face of the young royals of Europe now and her popularity was rival to that of the Queen of England.

Meanwhile back in Boldovia and at the VonStine Manor house, the Count and Baron were watching the television and the race. They could see Albert and Mary along with Edward and Tasha. "Hmmmm do you think Carmella will attack them while the race is going on" The Baron asked.

The Count shook his head "no dear boy she won't risk it there, I fear she will attack Boldovia itself and when she does it will be fast.

I have guards out all over the mountain just in case of an attack. We were ready last time and knew the VH men were coming. But this time I fear we will not have a warning and we will have to counter an attack. "The Count said as he smoked a pipe.

"Though I have to say Albert and Mary look like they are having a wonderful time in Monti Carlo. Just that wolf better keep them safe after all its his city and he did invite them. If something happens, I will never forgive him." The Count stated.

The Baron just nodded as he sat back sipping his beer. Which at that moment Lily walked in and sat on her husband's lap and looked over at her father.

"How is the race going and how is Albert and Mary doing so far." She asked.

The Baron smiled "the race has been a good one and Albert and Mary seem to be doing just fine for now." The Baron said to his wife.

They all sat and relaxed watching the race from the manor house. Finally, the race came to an end and as it did the Prince along with Mary and Albert came out to award the trophies. It was a fun moment and the camera's went off everywhere. In the end Albert and Mary were able to dodge the champagne bath from the ceremony.

As the race had ended Mary and the rest went back to the hotel to enjoy the late afternoon as they wanted. Which was back to the beach, and they would stay there for a few hours.

Night had come to the city of Monti Carlo and Demitriof was up and meeting with his men. As he sat in the safe house one after the others came in to give him the reports. Finally, his spy from inside the werewolf kings court came in to give a report.

A man in all black came in and bowed to Demitriof. "Good evening lord Demitriof it is good to see you again master. "He said.

Demitriof looked up from his chair and smiled. As Demitriof smiled you could see some blood still on his fangs. "Ah good evening, Marcus what news do you have for me." Demitriof said.

Marcus had a note binder and opened it up as he started his report. "Lord Demitriof the Wolf King Zagreus is set up in an old keep just on the outskirts near the beach. For our attack if I may suggest we move to attack from the beach there are three tunnels that are easy to access, and it's not heavily guarded as the rest of the keep." Marcus said.

Demitriof looked over the full folder and then looked at Marcus. "How many men do we have total?". Marcus looked over to a large Black man who was bald and in camo gear,

"Ron, how many men do you have here?" Marcus asked.

"I have fifty men ready to go just give the word, we will hit them before they know what hit them. Their main force is not at the keep so they should only have maybe thirty wolves there. "Ron replied.

Demitriof looked at both men, "Then let's move out I want to be ready for the Queen to show up. If we time this just right, then Mothers attack will take place at the same time." Demitriof said.

As Demitriof and his men were leaving and fixing to move on the king of the werewolves keep, back in the old capital of Teveahna, Morgan was stepping out of the safe house he was in his armor but hidden in a black trench coat, with a large bag which of course all his weapons were inside. Morgan heard a familiar voice and looked to his right. It was a smaller man with slightly grey hair. "Well boss good to see you here. Figured you would show up here with all the vampire activity going on. So, what's the mission?" The smaller man asked.

Morgan shook his head "Not this time Oscar this is not for the company and something I have to do alone."

Oscar nodded, "Right boss so what is the mission I don't have anything else to do and looks like you need some help. So, for one last ride let me come along. You know you need me." Oscar said.

Morgan sighed "Alright lets go I will fill you in as we head up to the castle." Morgan started to walk to the edge of the city and looked up the road to the castle.

Oscar nodded, "glad I have my armor on and I have my rifle and pistol right here along with my short bladed." Oscar told Morgan quietly.

Morgan keep looking around he knew Carmella's men were ready to move but he had to get to the castle before they did to evacuate everyone.

"Ok here is what is going on Oscar. I am working for Sek-Met and yes, I know hard to believe but true, I am to save the Queen and stop Carmella or die trying. Now when we get to the castle let me do the talking but I know they have some C4 in the garage area by the main guard house. So, get all you can get and wire the whole castle. I mean I want it so we can blow that thing sky high." Morgan said to Oscar.

Oscar was stunned. They were going thought on what he was just told.

"Boss a war is fixing to start isn't it." Oscar said as she sighed. "But if it's out last ride it's going to be one hell of a ride." Oscar finished saying.

Morgan nodded as he waves down a cab. "Yes, Oscar one last time, Remember follow my lead when we get to the castle." Morgan stated.

Oscar nodded "right Boss"

The cab stopped right beside the men, and Oscar loaded the bags. As Oscar loaded the gear into the back of the cab Morgan explained to the Driver who he was and where they were going. He also stated they had to get there fast. The cab driver at first did not believe the Morgan but when Morgan showed the crest on the letter he nodded to Morgan as the two men got in, he took off towards the castle. Morgan just hoped they would get there in time.

# 6

# John Meets With his Father

As night feel fell over Monti Carlo John, Rebecca and her pack were in the lobby with Mary and Albert and her guards along with Edward and Tasha. John looked at everyone.

"Alright everyone Rebecca and I are off to see my Father. I want all of you to stay here at the hotel till we get back don't do anything stupid. Do you understand Edward!" John said looking at Edward.

Edward nodded "Ok, Ok,, John I understand we will keep Mary and Albert safe. I Promise." Edward replied.

John looked at Edward with a not so trusting look on his face, but he had no choice in this matter. John turned and walked out of the Hotel with Rebecca and her pack right behind him. They walked down the steps to three waiting black cars. As Mary and her group watched.

The cars pulled away and went down the street, but Albert saw something out of place and as everyone went back into the lobby. Albert stopped everyone and told them what he saw.

"Mary, Edward wait, There are four men across the street they have trench coats on, but I saw one with a armor crest on his left side. They have to be part of the assassins we were to be looking out for." Albert told everyone.

Edward nodded to the pack members, and they went out the back. But of course, Mary was not staying behind and followed them. The group made it out the back of the hotel and went around the side. Mary was no fool nor was Albert and stayed back so the main soldiers of the pack could do their job. The soldiers spotted the men that Albert had said he had seen. Quietly the group stated to follow the five men.

John and Rebecca were in the first car as they were going through the city, it would not be a long ride for the city of Monti Carlo is not very large. But Rebecca looked over at her brother.

"John I am having a bad feeling not sure why, but something is off. I hope all is okay in Boldovia or stays okay till everyone gets back." Rebecca told her brother.

John looked out of the car and just nodded in agreement with what his sister just said. The night was clear, but Johns mind was not he had so many things going through his mind at the moment. His father had come for the weddings, but this was different. It was now going to be formal, and he did not know what his father was planning.

The three cars pulled up finally Infront of the old keep. It set on a rocky outcropping on the edge of the Mediterranean sea. It was built way back in the middle ages. Its entrance was somewhat like the Stines Castle with two different gates and a large walls going around it. As they walked through the gates, they came into a courtyard that lead to the main area of the keep.

As the doors opened John was met by his brother Travis. Travis was happy to see John and gave him a hug. John smiled and hugged his brother back. Travis smiled at Rebecca "Welcome home Sister good to see you finally brought John home." Tavis said jokingly to his sister.

Rebecca laughed as well. "Yes, took me forever to get him finally home. I take it father is waiting on him." Rebecca said.

Travis nodded "Yes, Father is in the main hall waiting on John. We better all go in you know how father will be if he is keep waiting."

With that the three of them went inside as Rebecca's pack stayed outside. The three of them would walk down a long hallway to two large doors. At the doors were two guards waiting for them. John took a deep breath and looked at his brother and sister and then motioned for the doors to open.

As John and his brother and sister walked into the room, they entered a massive round room with columns that went around the outer circle of the room. The center roof was a glass dome that was like a skylight and let the moonlight in. To the far side was a raised area with a large throne and at it right side a smaller throne. Sitting on the large throne was a Large man in a suit, his hair was grey, and he had a trimmed beard. His eyes blue in color and his face showed scars of battle from long ago. This was King Zagreus the king of the werewolves and John's father.

John walked towards his father with his brother and sister just behind him. Rebecca's pack came in from outside and fanned out to both sides with more men and women standing around near the columns. John bowed in front of his father. "Good evening, King Zagreus. It is good to see you father." John said paying respect to his father.

King Zagreus looked at his son. "Your late as usual John."

"I am not you said to be here at seven and is it not seven." John replied.

"No, it's not John you forgot the time difference between here and Boldovia again." King Zagreus said.

John had a look of shock on his face. "Oh... Sorry father I do apologize for that." John said.

"I figured as much. You have always been forget full John. Now let's get down to business. I am not happy with you over the fact that you have not visited or even come to see your mother and I in over what now sixty-five plus years. Also, what the hell happened with my great grandchildren all but what four are dead. I want to know exactly what the hell is going on in that country that it cost us those kids lives. I know I am to speak to that Queen of Boldovia, but she is so young and now with reports of Carmella and her people on the move." The King yelled.

"John listen we are getting reports that Carmella is massing near or in Boldovia with all her people. You have a war coming to Boldovia and I don't think the Count can win it." The King explained to John.

John just sighed. "Father, I know all this we know that Carmella has called for war on the country. But we can't go public as you know the whole world would go nuts if they knew that Vampires and Werewolves and other monsters were real. The panic would rock the world and you know it. Think of all the lives that would be lost on a massive monster hunt. "John told his father.

Rebecca looked at both of them "Father we know Mary got a deal with the United States and they are upgrading the military. I don't know how far they have gotten but they have gotten some new equipment. But even with our army we are so far away, and we only have five hundred men. There is nothing we can do. But the kids are here with the queen. So, if something happens soon, they are all here and safe." Rebecca said.

King Zagreus slammed his fist down on his throne "I don't care what we have. This is the Counts problem not mine, and for now my great grandchildren will stay here. I want them in the keep by morning, I will have a long talk with that Queen as well. This is getting way too hot for all of us, and I want it taken care of as soon as possible. I am tired of seen my family dead. Do I make myself Clear. "The king yelled.

John was stunned "Wait just a minute they are grown, and they are not your subjects they are Mary's. Now yes you best meet with her. But it is their choice on where they want to live and what to do. You know that they are not little pups anymore no matter how mad you get." John yelled at his father.

The King stood up and walked up to John and looked him eye to eye. Both did not back down it was like two alpha wolves staring down at each other and it was so intense that everyone in the room felt it. John did not back down.

The King growled. "John I am warning you."

John growled back "No father I am warning you. You remember my sons are still in Boldovia and my grandchildren are their children."

The King sighed "Alright John for now I will just talk with your Queen. But this is not over by a long shot." The King said.

"Alright Father for now we will wait till after your talk with Mary" John replied.

Meanwhile Mary's party was following the five men. Edwards pack keep a good eye on them. But something was not right as they followed them down by the beach. Edward pulled a stop as there was no way to stay hidden if they went any further. As they stayed out of view Tasha reminded everyone that they maybe Carmella's people and if so, might be some type of ghoul and vampires maybe involved and they have heightened senses at night.

As the group keep low and watched several boats came out of the darkness and they saw at least fifty men come on the beach all in black. There was three men that stood out. One was a tall build man with black hair he seemed to be the leader for the others were around him. The other two were big as well one was a bald black man and the second was a man with red hear. Edward made note of their body heat and it was colder than normal. They were like the count and had to be Vampires.

Demitriof looked at both Ron and Marcus "no mistakes we have to take the king and his court alive, his bodyguards they are a different story I want them eliminated. Mother has made her orders clear. So, no mistakes understood." Demitriof ordered.

With that all the men headed on the beach to the keep. They knew that there was a set of tunnels in the rock cliff that the keep sat on. Which would lead them deep into the keep and they planned on catching the whole keep off guard.

Edward looked at everyone. "Well, we heard them they plan on attacking the kings keep. What do you want to do Mary? They are monsters and you and Albert are going to be out matched. "Edward said in a very soft voice.

Mary smiled "oh I think Albert and I will be just fine, but I want that one who is in charge he has to be close to Carmella. So, we have to get him. "Mary said looking at Albert.

Albert just smiled. "been wanting to try this stuff out in a real fight. "Albert said to Mary.

Edward, Tasha, and the pack all looked at Mary and Albert. They were wondering what was going on. As Mary and Albert looked around.

"All Clear" Albert told Mary.

With that both of them looked at the group. "Let's go" Mary said.

With that Mary and Albert looked over to the pack as their armor started to wrap around them. Mary looked to Edward.

"Did you forget what I told you about our training and armor?" Mary said to Edward.

The Pack was shocked for It was the first time they saw Albert and Mary in their armor.

"Oh, right I forgot you two had armor now." Edward replied.

# 7

# Attack on the Court of the Wolf King

As Demitriof and his men approached the werewolves stronghold from the beach. Demitriof's men spread out to make sure no one was off to the sides to sound an alarm. Demitriof men were in sets of three as they fanned out on the beach. One team moved off to the left side of the beach where some large rocks were.

As they approached, they heard four men talking. The men were talking about the Kings oldest son had returned home and was meeting with the king. They were wondering if the Kings son would be taking over and the King step down. The men were not paying attention for they figured no one would attack the court.

Demitriof's men moved in silence and attacked the men catching them totally off guard. Demitriof's men took the men out quick and quietly. They then moved the bodies to an area out of sight.

More guards were walking the beach but again they were too busy talking than keep watch like they were support to. Which more of Demitriof's men would take advantage and again the guards would fall to the attackers.

While all this was going on the group that Mary and Albert were with finally made it up to the beach but keep a distance. Mary with her visor down over her helmet would easily see what was going on as could Albert. Edward, Tasha, and the pack were with them. They would make sure to stay hidden from behind. They could not do anything at the moment and had to wait. Even though more werewolf guards feel to Demitriof's men.

At the base fortress was six openings with two guards at each one. Demitriof looked over at Ron and nodded. With that motion Ron and several of his men moved in and flanked the men at the openings. Quietly they attacked. This time the Guards were not caught off guard as much as the others. Several of the men shifted forms but again Ron's men were on top of them all and killed all the men and werewolves. Ron and his men had keep things quiet just as planned so not to set off any alarm's. Demitriof walked to Ron and looked at all the dead.

"Very nice Ron. You did a great job. Now hide all these bodies we can't have anyone finding them and sound alarms, Also leave some men here to protect the entrances. I want a clear path to the beach, so we have no issues when we leave." Demitriof ordered.

"Yes, Lord Demitriof as you command." Ron replied.

At the entrances Demitriof looked over the layout of the stronghold and motioned for his men to head into all the tunnels, Ron's team would take the far-right tunnel while Marcus team would take the far left one. Demitriof would go in one of the middle ones.

From a distance Mary, Albert along with Edward, Tasha and the pack all watched staying well behind so on to get noticed. Edward looked at everyone. "Seemed like the big guy went down one of the middle tunnels but If I am guessing right, we should probably follow one of those two men he had with him. So, lets break into two teams, Team one goes to the right and team two goes left." Edward suggested.

Edward looked at everyone "Let's do this Albert you and Mary take half the pack and go down the far right side, We will go down the far left. Now don't do anything stupid. Wait till we all meet up and then pick when to act. Remember they are attacking John and the rest inside." Edward said.

Mary and Albert four of the pack soldiers agreed and took off to the far right tunnel. Edward and the rest went to the far left.

Mary and her team went quietly down the tunnel they had to be perfectly quiet for the men they were following were not making any sound.

Mary and Albert had no problem seeing the men in the solid black tunnel their armor game them the ability to see in total darkness. As they watched the men move it was clear they were just like those who attacked the Castle and killed their friends a couple of years ago.

Mary wanted vengeance so bad but knew she would have to wait it was more important to follow and if need be, aid and save John and the court here.

Demitriof's men finally made it to the entrance of the keep and found several guards around it. This would be tricky as they had to keep everything quiet.

The four men split into two teams of two and moved in. They hit the guards from behind and pulled them into the dark tunnel killing them by slicing the spine at the back of the neck. They then laid them down quietly in the tunnel. Two men would stay and guard the entrance as the other two would move forward into the keep.

As Mary and Albert got to the entrance, they all stopped and found two men had been left behind. The pack members with Mary and Albert were her elite army bodyguards. Her men stayed to the shadows and waited for the men to turn their backs to them and when they did the pack made fast work of them. They keep it quiet. So, no one would know they were following. As the group keep back, they could hear fighting up ahead of them do to how their helmets of the armor were.

Ron's team worked as six four men teams and worked just like those of the VH Corporation did when they attacked the mountain that night. So, for the pack it was well known, and they could hide without a problem from them as long as they stayed back and behind them.

Albert was up at the front with the pack. Even though Mary was in armor she was still the Queen and had to be protected. Mary did not like this but not much she could do about it. The pack was holding back as best they could, but they did not like watching the fighting and seeing the werewolves dropped by Ron's men.

As Ron's team finally came into one of the main hallways of the stronghold they would now have to spread out. Ron motioned for each team on which way to go. He had a copy of the layout of the stronghold and figured the King and court would be in the main hall in the middle if everything worked out, they could incircle and take the fight to them.

Meanwhile Marcus and his teams were making their way to the main hallways as well. Which was leading Edward Tasha and the rest of the pack as well. Edward had everyone stop and wait for there was so much movement out in the hallway. Both packs would sit and wait for now and let things take place so they could make a move if needed.

Demitriof finally came out into the main hallway and looked seeing all his men moving around. Ron and Marcus had met up with Demitriof. and nodded in agreement with how the operation was going. They waited till all the men were set and finally started walking towards the center of the stronghold. As his men had taken out all of the outer buildings guards. Demitriof was very pleased how everything was going and knew his mother would be happy that the werewolves were out of the picture before she moved on the Stines Castle and Boldovia.

Meanwhile in the heart of the stronghold John was still talking with his father and not happy about them taking Edward and Tasha into protective custody. Rebecca was trying to keep both men calm as they keep yelling at each other.

"You can't do this Father! Edward and Tasha are both adults and it should be their choice on if to stay here or go home with Albert and Mary !" John yelled at his father.

King Zagreus stood up in anger and walked over to John "Now you listen to me, you have always been disobedient to the family John, and you put my Great Grand Children in danger all the time. And I have had enough. No more they will stay here and if you push it so will you. I have had enough of this with those Vampires!" The King yelled.

At that moment alarms sounded, and everyone looked around. King Zagreus yelled "What the hell is going on guards!" But to his surprise only the guards in the central dome was seen and responded.

John looked to Rebecca "Get your pack ready for a fight looks like we are under attack!" John yelled.

But it was too late and as they were fixing to shift forms Demitriof, and his two aids came out with his men. Though it seemed only thirty of Demitriof's men came out. Ron had staged men in the main hallway just in case.

"Well, well what do we have here but a bunch of mutts. Have to say it was way too easy for my men to take this stronghold. Cannot believe you only had that many guard here. Tisk, Tisk foolish King Zagreus." Demitriof said.

"Who are you... Vampire?" King Zagreus screamed seeing the body heat off Demitriof.

Demitriof smiled "Ah very good King, I am Demitriof Valmor youngest son of the Duchess Carmella Valmor Tempish. "Demitriof proclaimed.

John growled "Your that Bitches son!"

Demitriof looked sternly at John. "say that again and I will personally kill you. But before that you will tell me where your Queen is." Demitriof stated.

John just smirked. "She was out on the town so no clue which means you don't have her do you." John said smiling.

Demitriof smirked "Oh it won't be long then and when I get her you can bet I will...." Demitriof was cut off from finishing what he was fixing to say. When behind him he heard a female voice speak up.

"And exactly what are you going to do to me you leaching piece of garbage. "Mary said.

Demitriof along with Ron and Marcus turned to see in shock Mary standing there behind them. She was not in her armor and looked like she had just come from the beach. Mary smiled at John and winked. John knew that Mary did not come alone and looked to his sister and blinked and nodded just a tad. Rebecca saw John and gave two hand signals to her pack that was behind her. As they all watched.

King Zagreus was shocked in seeing the Queen how did she just show up what was going on. But then he saw his son and daughter and the pack and smiled in understanding and put his hand on the hilt of his sword and waiting for the right moment.

Demitriof smiled "well look what we have here the lovely Queen of Boldovia, Mary Jade VonStine, how nice to finally meet you my dear cousin. "Demitriof said. As he looked to Marcus who pulled out an iPad. Marcus turned it on and hit the video conference app on it. On the screen was Carmella herself.

Carmella smiled seeing Mary "Ah hello my lovely niece it is so good to see you again. While my son has you their all tied up, I am fixing to attack your family and I mean to take over this city and destroy everything you hold dear. So yes, war is now here, and I have won. Demitriof make sure she doesn't leave that stronghold alive." Carmella said.

"Yes Mother, I am going to enjoy this." Demitriof said as he looked at Mary.

"Carmella, one thing before you go." Mary said.

Carmella smiled at Mary, "Yes Mary what is it?"

"Who said I came alone" Mary said as Albert came out in all his armor. Mary looked at the vampires.

Carmella screamed "What the hell they are forbidden from getting involved even Horus can't get involved what the hell is he doing there. Demitriof kill them now."

Marcus dropped the iPad at which point Mary's armor appeared around her and the pack charged out towards the Vampires. This was the signal for John and Rebecca's pack to act and they all shifted and attacked. Demitriof and his men were caught in between the two forces.

Demitriof could not believe what he was seeing as Mary looked like Bastet or her armor did and before he could do much Mary clawed him making him fall back and roll to come back up with his sword drawn.

"Who the hell are you, you're not human and you're not like us? "Demitriof yelled at Mary as he charged her.

Mary was focused and on point as her armor on her arm blocked Demitriof's sword strike. "I am my mother's daughter" Mary yelled as her claw just missed Demitriof's chest.

Ron instead of backing up charged into Albert catching him and running back into one of the outer pillars. They went through the pillar, but Albert was able to absorb the hit with his armor and roll with it.

As Albert got up, he pulled his swords from his back and looked at Ron. Ron smiled as he had pulled the axe from his back for, he had not had a good fight in a long time. "You're not Horus so who the hell are you?" Ron yelled.

Albert keep up his attack on Ron "I am the Queen's Husband" Is all Albert said. His swords were slowly taking bits out of Ron's axe and Ron could see it. Ron could not figure out why it was happening and why the swords of his enemy were not even scratched. But it did not matter for Ron turned the axe and hit albert with the flat side knocking him through another pillar.

Edward and Rebecca both attacked Marcus while John and Tasha keep the King safe fighting the other Vampire warriors. The King was not one to stay out of a fight and was right in the middle of things, but he keep looking over at Mary and Albert and trying to figure out what was going on and why she looked so much like Bastet and who was the one that looked like Horus.

"John when this is over you got some explaining to do about that Queen of yours. "The King yelled as he ran his sword though one of the vampires.

John just laughed even though he was in his wolf warrior form and was in the middle of ripping a vampire into as many pieces as he can.

The fight was total chaos but contained in the main hall. But as many Vampires had fallen so did Werewolves. Mary and Albert along with the rest knew they had to get this fight over with fast, but Demitriof and his two commanders were just too tough, and they had to really work to beat them.

Demitriof had cut down two werewolves trying to keep distance between him and Mary. But he started to figure out her move set and started to counter her.

Though Mary was fast, and angel Demitriof could now tell how she moved and finally caught her.

"Finally caught you!" Demitriof yelled.

But Albert had been keeping an eye on her he threw one of his swords spooking Demitriof making him let go of Mary.

Demitriof screamed at Ron "Kill him now !"

Mary looked over for a moment at Albert. Just as Ron ran into him and again running him though another pillar. But that's all the time Demitriof needed and finally was able to hit Mary,

Mary went flying towards Albert. But she was able to land on her feet. Mary looked up at Demitriof in what looked like some kind of three-point stance. Albert stood up behind her holding one sword. As they took a breath. Ron walked over by Demitriof.

"These two are a pain. It makes no sense they are just human right?" Ron asked Demitriof.

While Ron was talking with Demitriof, Marcus was tied up with Edward, Tasha, and the pack they had him isolated from the rest. Demitriof pointed to Marcus "Ron help Marcus I can handle these two." Demitriof said.

Demitriof was getting upset now and aggressively attacked Mary and Albert. Albert still had not recovered his second sword and had to perry Demitriof's first sword strike. Mary had slide to the side and came around with her claws and just missed hitting Demitriof in the side.

Ron looked back at Demitriof and then turned back around and ran over to the area that Marcus and the pack was but as he got closer to the group John hit him from the side sending him into a wall.

Demitriof ran at Mary and Albert but as he did Mary and Albert split going opposite directions. Demitriof was thrown off for a moment but then he got back on track and keep his focus on Mary but an eye on Albert. For when he went for a hit on Mary, Albert would come in from the side and Demitriof would have to perry his sword attack and then pull back dodging Mary's claws.

Demitriof could not get an advantage in fact he was on his heels just staying on defense at the moment for Mary and Albert were moving just as they had been trained and Demitriof just could not find an opening to counterattack. For now, Demitriof would have to wait for a moment to attack.

John was moving towards Ron and as Ron stood up, he saw Marcus in trouble and tried to rush to his aid, but John went after him, and his claw just missed Ron. Ron turned around and was able to land a punch up against Johns head knocking him over to a wall. John was getting up when Rebecca came at Ron form the Side. Ron had just enough time to dodge to the left but doing so he was out of place and at that moment Edward finally got a clean hit on Marcus with a powerful claw strike. Marcus was knocked down. Edward was on him, and his fangs ripped into Marcus neck and shoulder killing him.

Ron screamed and had rage in his eyes. "Marcus ... No! ... I will kill you all I swear it!" Ron was blinded by rage.

Demitriof yelled "Ron behind you !"

Ron turned but he was caught flat footed as John had made it behind him. As Ron looked at John. Rebecca's claw came across and hit true, slicing Ron's neck clean through. Ron took a step back and then feel his head rolling off his shoulders.

Demitriof could not believe what he was seeing his men dead and his loyal retainers Marcus and Ron both defeated his rage ran though him as he started to charge towards John and Rebecca, but he had made one fatal mistake and lost sight of Mary and Albert.

Mary came in from the left side of Demitriof and slid up under him her claw struck him right below his breastbone, and it brought Demitriof to a stop. Demitriof shook as his breath was shallow and fast as if having an anxiety attack. Mary's claw was up under Demitriof's breastbone holding his heart. Demitriof looked down at Mary but could not move. Mary helmet retracted as she looked up at Demitriof. "Goodbye Cousin" was all Mary said. Mary's claw crushed Demitriof's heart killing him and letting him drop to the ground. It was the first time Mary had personally taken anyone's life.

Mary stood there shaking just a little as Albert came over to her and put his arm around her. "You did what you had to do. It's okay take a deep breath it's not over yet. Carmella is out there somewhere. "Albert said to Mary.

Mary nodded as she looked over at everyone. John and the others were checking on the wounded and making sure that the vampires were all dead. Rebecca came over to her father and checked on him. The king was fine but was looking at Mary and Albert and their armor they were in. As everyone had gathered around the king in the center of the main hall.

# 8

# Morgan Rescues the
# Royal Guard

The cab pulled up in front of the Castle. As it did several of the guards came out and approached it. Just then Morgan got out. The Captain of the guards along with four guards surrounded Morgan.

The Captain of the guards looked at Morgan with a stern look. "Who are you and what are you doing this area is off limits to the public?" The Captain said.

Morgan took out Sek-Mets letter out and gave it to the Captain. "This will explain everything. But after you read it call every man you have out for battle. This is not a drill, and I will explain what is going on." Morgan said to the Captain.

The Captain read the letter his eyes went wide as he did and turned to the guards that were with him. "You herd what he said now get everyone up and ready for battle. NOW!" The Captain yelled.

The Guards yelled "Yes sir!"

As the guards took off to the castle the Captain looked at Morgan. "I am sorry Sir Morgan; I did not know the Queen had picked her Knight. We are all at you command." The Captain said as he walked Morgan to the gate, Morgan looked back and yelled at Oscar to get the gear. Oscar was right behind Morgan as they went into the Castle.

Morgan looked to the Captain. "I need to know how many men we have and who else is in the castle. So, all info you can give me I need to know.it as soon as possible. Also, what do we have that's flammable. I need that information fast." Morgan asked.

The Captain looked at Morgan with a strange look but started going over everything with him. To Morgan's shock the Americans were still here which was the worst case possible.

Morgan shook his head. "Get everyone up get everyone dressed and down to the tunnels going to the keep and I mean now. "Morgan ordered.

Morgan looked over at Oscar. "Oscar, you heard the Captain. The gas reserve is in the garage wire it to blow up I want to take as many of those bastards as we can when they get past the gate." Morgan said. Two guards looked at Morgan and Oscar. Oscar looked to the guards. "Well, you heard his orders lets go" Oscar said as they walked to the garage.

Morgan stood by the tree thinking he was not liking this, but he had to get everyone to safety. He knew his time was limited and in about three hours they were going to attack or that was his guess. For the sun would be down and darkness is a vampires alley.

The guards ran though the castle waking everyone up, David and his wife and the Judge were all woken up and told to get dressed fast. They had no idea what was going on but followed the guards. As they got into the elevator it did not stop at the floor and keep going. It would take about five minutes to get to the bottom of the shaft.

As the elevator opened the Phillips and the Judge were met by guards and lead down the tunnel till, they got to the keep. As they came out in the keep, they found Guards all around in full combat gear and taking up defensive positions at the outer walls of the keep.

David stopped a guard. "What's going on?" David asked.

The Guard looked at David and said. "We have intel that a major attack is coming, and we had to evacuate the castle. I am sorry sir that's all I can tell you at this time. The First Knight is in charge of everything and when he gets here you can ask him. "the guard said.

David was not happy and asked if there was any more gear in the keep, he could have he was ex-military and active law enforcement in the states. The guard nodded and showed him to the armory.

Crystal saw David come out in full battle gear looking over the MAK-90 assault rifle, as he was not used to working with one. David looked up seeing his wife and smiled. "Well seems those who wanted Mary dead are not all dead. And it looks like were in the middle of it." David said to Crystal.

Crystal shook her head and walked over to her husband and took the nine-millimeter pistol off his side and looked it over and inspected it. "You think I am not going to be armed for this your nuts. And you remember this you better come back to me. Or I swear to God if you die, when I die, I will come and kick your ass." Crystal said.

David smiled and kissed his wife "I am not dying, and I am going to finish this for Victor and Isis." David said to his wife.

David got another pistol, and one guard gave the Judge one as well. The Judge just shook his head. "Well David, here we go again. I am getting to old for this crap." The Judge said. David nodded to the Judge as he went out with the Guards.

Back in the castle the Guards that remained were all in battle gear and ready to fight. Morgan looked around and looked over at the two guards up on the battlement.

"Ok men. I am Jay Lester Morgan; I am the Queens First Knight. This man beside me is Oscar Galidoran, he is my assistant so if he gives you an order follow it like its myself giving the order. Now let's get down to what is fixing to happen. Down in the city I know Carmella is there. Not just that but she has an army of at least five hundred vampires and ghouls all loyal to her. They will soon attack the mountain and the city. We have to make it look as though everyone dies up here. So, we are going to blow up the castle. Now when that happens, I want to take as many of them as we can. So, everyone get with Oscar to wire the whole castle. "

The Captain looked to Morgan "Sir, we will need to have some men stay behind. It's a suicide mission but it has to be done or they will key in on what were up to." The Captain said to Morgan.

Morgan sighed and looked to the thirty-five men that was still at the castle. "Dam it. I need ten volunteers. I need men who have had children your families must live on to keep your memories." Morgan said.

The guards stepped forward. One guard looked to Morgan. "Sir we are all Ghouls of the Count we have lived over one hundred years and our children and descendants are numerous so we will stay and fight to the end. "The guard said.

Morgan nodded in understanding. "Ok Oscar get the guards and the C-4 and let's get this castle wired you got thirty minutes at most so get to it." Morgan ordered

Oscar took over and got everyone to get C-4 and went over how to set the wireless control timers. At that point everyone started to move out and wire the castle fully. Morgan went to the battle mount and looked out at the city. He wished he could call the Count, but he knew Carmella's men would be monitoring all communications on the mountain. Morgan just hoped he had enough time.

Meanwhile in the pass where the trains ran from the capital to the city of Teveahna, fifty of Carmella's soldiers were set up and planting explosives to cut off the city. For the road and train traveled though this one pass, With it cut off the city and the castle was helpless. They waited for the word as they had all the explosives set up.

But Carmella changed her mind and gave them a new order to blow up the pass as the train came into it. So right on time the Train came though the pass and then it happened.

A massive explosion went off that could be seen a heard all the way to the castle. Morgan knew that this was it. He turned and looked down at Oscar. "Were out of time Oscar" Morgan yelled.

Oscar signaled all was ready and waiting for Morgan to come down. Morgan arrived as all the guards made it to the main foreyard. Morgan sighed.

"Ok men time to go, Captain, you have everyone's names who are staying." Morgan said

The Captain nodded. "Yes Sir" he said.

The Captain gave Morgan the list and looked at him. The Captain just smiled. "Can't come with you, I have to stay and give orders till the end. My wife is long dead, I will finally rest with her. My great grand-children will be fine. Give them this note for me sir. "The Captain told Morgan.

Morgan saluted the men "You will be the heroes we all remember. Take as many of those bastards as you can. I promise we will win this war and Carmella will die. And Mary will always be our Queen." Morgan proclaimed.

The ten guards took up positions with the Captain of the Guards with them as Morgan, Oscar, and the guards left to the keep. It was now up to the guards and Morgan just prayed that those in the Manor house would live though all this, but he did all he could and what he was asked to do.

As The rest of the guards and Morgan came out of the tunnel to the keep, they found it fully manned and defended. But what Morgan was not ready for was David Phillips in battle gear.

"And exactly what are you doing Sherriff Phillips "Morgan said

David looked to Morgan. "Who are you to ask what I am doing."

Morgan realized he was not in his gear and looked at David. "I am the Queens First Knight Jay Lester Morgan, and I am in charge of this operation. Now again exactly what are you doing?" Morgan said in a stern voice.

David looked at Morgan "I want a piece of those Basterds who killed my best friend and threatens his daughter. Now you want to butt heads or what" David said.

Morgan remembered the file on David and his military record. "Alright Sargent Phillips, First Calvary Division, Grey Wolves right" Morgan said.

David was surprised "Your intel is correct. Morgan, was it?" David said.

Morgan shrugged "Ok just your under my orders and no mistakes we only get one shot at this. For now, we hold up here and wait for re-inforcements." Morgan explained.

David, Oscar, and the guards all looked at Morgan "Reinforcements from where they just blew up the pass!" they all said.

Morgan shrugged again "All I know is we have help on the way and to wait." Morgan said but in truth he really did not know.

# 9

# Mary and the Wolf King of Monaco

Back at the werewolf keep King Zagreus was furious as he paced back and forth as his throne room was being cleaned up of all the dead, The King punched his throne over and over. "They dare to attack my kingdom; Carmella has gone way to far she is going to pay for this attack. "The King screamed.

Rebecca tried to calm her father down. "Father please calm down we have to regroup first." Rebecca said

King Zagreus screamed at his daughter "Calm down, Calm down they killed my son's and your brothers." The King then turned and looked at Mary and Albert who were still in armor but without the helmets on. "And you two, you two, What the hell is going on and who or what the hell are you two. I want answers now!" The King Screamed.

Mary looked to John for a moment "You want to tell him, or should I explain" Mary said to John.

John shook his head "Oh no this is all yours, your majesty. "John said not wanting his dad to yell at him.

Mary walked towards the King "Very well I will explain. As you know I am Queen Mary Jade VonStine and I rule Boldovia, This is my Husband Albert Ludwig VonStine." Mary said pointing to Albert. "I am sure you know of the war between The Count and Carmella," Mary said.

The King was starting to calm down Mary's voice was calming him down, but he was still wanting to know what was going on.

Mary continued. "You know about my Father Victor VonStine and his connection to the VonStine Throne, But you do not know about my mother Isis VonStine. "Mary took a deep breath for now she had to tell her secret.

"My mother is the daughter of …. The Goddess Bastet… Whose Husband is the God Anubis. That is why I have the armor and I have claws. This is why my parents were murdered by the VH Corporation. The Lee family of England are monster hunters, and my mother was their target to kill. My Husband made a pact with Horus and became his Paladin to keep me safe and to protect me." Mary said.

Everyone there expect for John and the original pack members and Edward, Tasha, and Albert. Were totally shocked and stunned at what Mary had just said. The King just sat down on his throne and looked at Mary and Albert.

"You're their granddaughter, you're like the old legends from Greece a real demi-god. I thought my late Great Grandfather was a liar. He claimed to be Hades son, but I never believed him. But here you both are. I wondered at your wedding why you had that aura about you. Now I understand. "the King sighed as he spoke. He then looked at John.

"And you knew about this all this time and did not tell me or even your sister." The King asked.

John looked to his father. "I had to keep her safe father it was the only way. I am not sorry for what I did, but it's done, and you know. Now what do we do now is the question." John said

Mary was thinking "Oh God Carmella is in the capital she is fixing to attack we have to get back to the castle." Mary said panicking.

Albert hugged Mary "Calm down Mary, we are nowhere near home, and we have to think this through. We are only fifteen strong, We are no match for a full-size army. Remember you beefed up the country's army so they should be able to stop her or hold her off till something can be done. "Albert told Mary.

Mary just shook her head not knowing what to do. She looked around at everyone knowing what they had just been through and still there was so much more to come.

# 10

# Hades and the Werewolf Army

Near an underground lake a cloaked figure stands. Before the figure the water is like a mirror and the cloaked figure watches what is going on in the werewolf stronghold. As the figure watches it turns and walks away.

As this cloaked figure keeps walking what looks like undead all line up in what looks like ancient armor from different time frames in history. As the cloaked figure nears what looks like a throne there standing beside the throne is a beautiful woman dressed in black silk robes. She has flowing red hair and blue eyes; Her skin is white as snow almost a feel of unnatural.

She watches the cloaked figure sit on the Throne. Her eyes look at the cloaked figure and with a very soft voice says. "What are you planning my love?" she asks.

"I have about had enough of that Cat and the rest of those from the sands. They know the law's and keep breaking them. I think it's time I put my foot down once and for all." The Cloaked man said as he stood up and started to walk to a river and a boat waiting for him. The red headed lady followed behind him.

In the main hall of the werewolf stronghold a large television was set up and they had the news on. Mary saw the report of the pass to her city getting blown up and almost lost it. But Albert was there to keep her in check.

"Relax Mary we can't do anything so no point in getting upset or out of control" Albert told her in a whisper. Mary nodded in understanding.

The warriors and others in the stronghold were working on all the wounded. John and Rebecca were with their father talking on what they could do next. It was very out of control at the moment. No one really had any idea's on what could be done to get everyone to Boldovia in time.

For some reason both Mary and Alberts armor put their helmets on without them thinking. Thankfully the armors did activate as without warning both Mary and Albert went flying into the television. Everyone turned to see who or what did it and standing there was the black cloaked figure and the lady with red hair.

"I have had enough of you Egyptian Gods coming into my territory and causing problems. No more this ends now. "the cloaked figure screamed.

Mary and Albert rolled just in time to avoid the clocked figures attack but just barely. Mary did not wait for him to attack again and went on the offensive and tried to hit the cloaked figure but missed and missed badly. The cloaked figure caught Mary and pinned her to the ground.

"Your very sloppy Bastet, you have never been like this in a fight, What happened did you just sit around all day or what? Also, where is that sister of yours." The cloaked figure said.

At that moment Albert was on him but only was able to get a hold of his cloak and pull it off of him. Which ended up wrapping around Albert and pinning him to the ground as if caught in a trap.

"Horus what is with you, You are worse than Bastet here is. "The now uncloaked man said,

Mary moved to protect and get Albert free, and her eyes were keep on the strange man. The man now uncloaked stood there looking down at them. He was around seven feet tall, He had long white hair and his skin was white and pale in color. His eyes were black and night.

"Great Hades stop!" The King yelled as he went and got in front of Mary and Albert. "Please listen they are not Bastet and Horus, and they came here to rescue all of us. Please stop." The King was begging Hades to stop.

Hades looked down at Mary and Albert as their helmets pulled back to show who they were. "Who are you two? "Hades asked.

The King sighed a sign of relief. "I will explain great Hades. This is The Queen of Boldovia and her Husband, they came as an invitation for their honeymoon. We were under attack by the vampire Carmella's son and his men. They came with my son John and his pack to aid in defending the stronghold." The King explained.

While the King talked to Hades the red haired lady came over and helped Mary get Albert untied.

"My husband can be very hot tempered from time to time." She said.

Mary looked at the beautiful red haired woman. "Your husband then that means your "The red haired woman cut Mary off "Yes, I am Persephone, and these here are out decedents from our son long ago." Persephone told Mary.

Mary looked to the King and was shocked for a moment. "And you said you thought demi-gods were fake and you're the ancestor was a godling like my mother was. "Mary said to the king.

The King did not know any of this and looked to Hades and to Persephone. "This is all news to me; I knew there was some kind of connection but not this." The King said.

Hades looked to the King "That can wait, I want to know how they have that armor" Hades said to the King.

The King sighed. "This is Mary Jade VonStine Queen of Boldovia, Her mother was Isis VonStine. Isis is the Daughter of Bastet, So Mary is her Granddaughter. That is why she has the armor. "The King said.

Hades thought for a moment "VonStine, isn't that the vampire kingdom." Hades stated as he looked around at the dead vampires. "But these are not VonStine vampires, are they?" Hades finished.

Mary stood up. "No, they are all part of Carmella's army which at this moment is attacking my home country. "Mary said to Hades.

Hades looked at Mary and then looked at the King, "Carmella has attacked my children and from what I understand from that Jackal God rules on her war with that vampire count. That is against his orders in which that now allows myself and in turn you to get involved." Hades says as he looked at the werewolf king.

Mary was shocked and looked from Hades to the King of the werewolves. "Um what does that mean?" Mary asked in a kind of shocked voice.

The King smiled "Rebecca summon every warrior we have and have them be ready for war. We will meet on the beach at the keep. Send word to the Prince of Monico and tell him what is going on. So just in case he has to do some public relations." The King said looking to his daughter.

Rebecca smiled and turned to her pack. "You heard the king let's get going now. "Rebecca yelled as her pack took off with Rebecca right behind them.

Edward and Tasha walked over to Mary and Albert. "So, what's the plan this time." Edward asked.

"Not sure but we have some new allies it would seem." Mary said to Edward.

Persephone walked over to her husband. "Beloved even with all the warriors how are you planning on getting them all to that kingdom?" She asked.

Hades just smiled at his wife. "I have a plan it will be fine I can guaranty it." Hades said with a wicked smile on his face as he looked at Mary.

Rebecca's pack would go throughout the countryside calling all the wolves to war. Rebecca would go to the Prince and inform him of all that happened and that the wolves were going to war. Though the Prince was in somewhat of shock he understood and gave his blessing.

The King along with the rest of the warriors in the keep along with Hades, Persephone, Mary and Albert and her people headed to the beach to wait for the rest. Though Mary was still not sure what Hades had planned all she could do was hope and pray they would get home in time.

Hades looked over at Mary, "You seemed troubled young one do not worry you will have your chance to face Carmella that I can promise you." Hades said to Mary.

Mary tried to smile but it wasn't working. "Thank you for your help." Mary said.

Albert rubbed Mary's back to help her calm down and relax while they waited for everyone. They would not have to wait long as each member of Rebecca's pack returned with warriors. With Rebecca finally returning. She would go right to her father.

"Father, I bring word from the Prince. He has given his blessing to go to war and destroy the Vampires of Carmella." Rebecca said loudly so all could hear.

Hades smiled as did the King and all around for now all was set and a army of werewolves ready for battle stood ready for war.

# 11

# Attack on Teveahna

The pass explosion followed by the train explosion rocked Teveahna. Chief Ludwig woke his wife and children and told them to get into the basement and stay there. His wife did not ask questions they like most of the citizens knew one day an attack would come just like the Count had told the city many years ago and it had put in a plan for this day.

Everyone in the city knew what to do and they put the Counts plan into action. All the homes had a secret place to hide in that was safe and everyone went into these basements.

The city police officers who were not on duty went to a wall closet and got their armor and weapons out and prepared for battle. They were police but also trained solders that trained with the royal guards in the past to be prepared for a attack. Every officer now moved out staying in the shadows. They would all meet up at the Cathedral and use it as a base of operations.

The Chief made sure his family was well hidden and then snuck out of the back of the house. He had to stay out of sight even though he was a tall man. His officers all knew what to do and as they moved, they could see all of the vampires moving though the city. The vampires had already taken the middle of the town fast. The Chief could not believe how fast and quiet they had moved. As the vampires were moving around the center of town several officers were at City Hall and Police station and there was where the fighting was. The men were putting up a good fight and the vampires were at moment pinned down. That is until a large man with black hair came out into the square, and he had several men around him in black armor.

To the side of this man was a smaller man about five foot six with short black hair. The smaller man looked up to the big man and said. "Sir Greggor we have some small resistance at city hall. What are your orders?"

Greggor looked down at the smaller man "Joshua blow it up, I want them all dead. Now get moving." Greggor said as he looked around. Something was wrong. "Where are all the people, where are all the police it makes no sense. "Greggor thought as he keep looking around.

As the vampires focused on the police station more officers made it to the cathedral . The officers all came in from the back and meet down under the main stage. Chief Ludwig looked around making note of all the men he had. Most of the force was here and ready for battle. So, he now had to just wait for a signal to counter this attack. Ludwig just felt bad for his men that was in the police headquarters and knew it was a lost cause.

"Captain how many men do we have?" The Chief asked one of his men.

"We have eighty nine men Chief. Only the night shift is at the main station sir." The captain said.

The Chief just sighed as he knew who the men on duty and knew he would lose them all.

Joshua and several men moved up staying behind the big statue. As Joshua and his men stayed pinned down behind the big statue of the late prince and Mary's father, Joshua looked at one of his men and motioned for him to place explosives around the statue.

As the explosives were being set Joshua's men finally had a chance to set up for an attack and one using an anti-tank weapon fired it at the police headquarters. There was a massive explosion at the front of the building sending flames skyward and knocking Joshua's men back off their feet. As they stood up, they could see half of the whole front of the building was blasted away.

Inside of the police station men were getting back up as they recovered but many more lay dead inside. The fire inside was spreading fast and moving towards all the officers inside.

Fire roared out of the opening. Officers had to come out due to the smoke and were shot on the spot killing all of them. Joshua looked over at Greggor for orders. Greggor motioned everyone to move forward and take city hall and the rest of the square. Greggor still felt uneasy as it was like the center of town was all abandoned.

Meanwhile in the capital at the main military base and on the tarmac, men dressed as mechanics moved into the hangers and found the F-35s. They moved back and forth quietly sabotaging them all. They got the first set of fighters disabled and moved to the second hanger. But as they did two guards saw them and sounded the alarm.

The alarms went off all over the base. The men quickly took out the guards and keep moving they still had to do their job. As soldiers came out of the barracks, they were shot at by the men dressed as mechanics. Each mechanic split up and went to a different hanger. The Soldiers fired their MAK-90's and they hit every man that was attacking. But the men did not fall, and the soldiers could not figure out why they were not dropping.

More and more soldiers come out firing at the men. The men know they will not escape and as they get into the hangers, they set of the explosives they had on their bodies. Each hanger explodes taking out all the aircraft in the hangers.

The Prime Minister was rocked out of bed and screams for his aid. "What the hell is going on!" He yelled.

His aid ran into the bedroom as the Prime Minister was standing up. His wife was sitting up in bed. "Sir the airbase is under attack all our aircraft have been destroyed. "The Prime Minister's Aid said.

The Prime Minster was blowing a gasket as he grabbed the phone and found no signal. "What communications are cut off as well. What is going on?" He asked.

General Pamitrioff was at the base and getting reports of what was going on. As he looked at the gate, he saw the Prime Minister's car pulled through the gates. General Pamitrioff took a deep breath as the cars pulled up and the Prime Minister and his cabinet got out. You could tell the Prime Minister was mad his face was red, and he was stomping over to the General.

"I want to know what the hell is going on and I want to know now!" The Prime Minister yelled at the General.

General Pamitrioff sighed again "We are under attack by what looks to be vampires. Our men are now inspecting the base and going building to building looking for more. We have lost all our aircraft except the eight super cobra's that are on their way back from doing training in Germany, but they are still hours away." The General told the Prime Minister.

The Prime Minister was pacing back and forth and looked over to his aid. "Do we have any communication's with the outside world, and what of the Queen and her party are they safe?" The Prime Minister said to everyone around him.

The General looked to his men "Well do we know if not let's find out and I mean now" The General told his men.

Everyone took off in different directions, as they tried to find answers for the Prime Minister and General. It was going to be a long night. And everyone was wondering what was going on in the city of Teveahna and if everyone was alright.

Several solders came up to the General and gave him several notes each. The General looked over all the notes and had a look of concern. "All the attacks are dead, but all were dead already most likely ghouls or vampires like what the count has on the mountain protecting the Queen. But they all have a different coat of arms on their uniforms." He told the Prime Minister.

The Prime Minister was shocked. "What do you mean different coat of arms? Show me right now!" The Prime Minister yelled.

The general looked over as two soldiers came up and showed them the crest that they found on the uniforms. The Prime Minster and General looked at the crest. Then they looked at each other. "This is bad you know what this means general?" The Prime Minster asked.

The general nodded. "Yes, Prime Minister it's the crest of the Bloody Countess just like the Count had warned us about. It looks like she finally is making her move. The army is already now on alert, and we will head out towards the old capital as fast as we can."The General said, as a solider brought him a new message.

The General Looked at the new message "Oh just great. The pass to Teveahna has been destroyed and it seems the trains were caught in the blast at moment there is no way we can get to the city. "The general told the Prime Minster.

The Prime Minster almost passed out. "Oh God no." The Prime Minster said as he found a place to sit down.

Greggor was on the steps with his men as he looked around seeing the city under their control now. But still could not find most of the police and the downtown area seemed to be abandoned. Greggor looked over at his men. "Time for the attack on the mountain get the men moving. I want everyone on that mountain dead. But bring me the Count, his wife, the Baron and Baroness, the rest kill. Now get going!" Greggor ordered.

"Joshua leave a squad of men behind I want them to look for the rest of the police and kill all of them." Greggor told Joshua.

Joshua looked over at the men who had taken out the Police Station. "Okay you guys you heard the boss get moving find the rest of the police and eliminate all of them." Joshua ordered.

The squad moved out leaving Greggor and Joshua along with the rest of Carmella's army. They had a job to do, and they were going to make sure to find the rest of the police and make sure they were dead.

# 12

# Attack on the VonStine Manor

Greggor looked to Joshua and nodded. "Go and make sure that nothing goes wrong. No slip ups this time. Mother will not accept failure in any way. "Greggor said to Joshua.

Joshua nodded and moved out with the men. Joshua was a head shorter than almost every man that was in Carmella's army. But you could tell all the men know his station and did not question him.

The armored vehicles pulled up into the square. They had been hidden in several safe houses around town that Carmella's army had held up in. Joshua and the men climbed into the vehicles and rolled out.

Joshua looked at his men in the armored vehicle he was in. "Remember we want the Count, Countess ,Baron, and Baroness alive. The Count, Countess and Baroness are all Vampires. The Count is a Master Vampire like Prince Tempest. The Countess and Baroness are equal to Lady Carmella in power. So, we have to be cautious when in combat with them. The Baron is something else not really alive or dead. So, no mess ups got it." Joshua told his men.

Meanwhile up at the Manor house the explosion could be heard and seen. The Count had everyone on alert and waiting for what was to come. Lily informed her father that she could not contact the castle. The Count knew that most likely they were evacuating everyone through the tunnels and the Count and those of the manor house would have to buy them some time.

The Count looked to the Baron, Lily and Mina and signed. "It looks like your sister is finally making her move. We have to stand and fight and give the castle time to evacuate we have to hold out as long as we can. Remember Mary is safe away from here. We can go all out without worry. Don't hold back take as many as you can with you and remember. I love you all and we are family no matter what happens remember that. "The Count said to everyone.

Everyone started to get ready for combat, The guards in the house went out by the main gates and set up tripwires that if the gates were moved would blow the whole front fence wall. The rest of the maids and servants got rifles and also set explosives into the elevator shaft. The Count picked up his sword and looked to his wife and daughter. The Baron picked up his war hammer he had gotten from Tarija's Brother.

As the Count looked out the window his eyes could see everything at night. He wondered if Mary was alright and safe. He thought of the humans in the castle and hoped they were evacuated and did Chief Ludwig and his men do as they had been told and were safe in the cathedral in town.

It was all he could do was think on those things and wait for the attackers. But his wait would not be long as he started to see men come near the gate to the manor house.

The Count moved back into the main study and motioned for everyone to get ready. Just then they all heard the gate explosives go off as the trip wires were touched.

As the gate exploded Joshua just shook his head, "Can't get good men these days. But oh well I have lots more" He said as he pointed his men to attack.

Joshua's men rushed through the gates in teams of six spanning out to move around the manor house. Five teams rushed the front doors firing though the doors with armor piercing bullets. The bullets shredded the wood of the doors to pieces.

When the teams got right at the doors a massive explosion went off and every member went flying back as shrapnel flew everywhere, Joshua just shook his head and pointed at the walls at the sides of the doors and looked at two of his men. "Blow those walls."

Four men came up and pulled up Laz rockets. The rocks hit the walls next to what was left of the doorway and exploded. Then more men rushed inside.

You could hear all the fire from the rifles go off and then yells inside. Joshua just walked up to the steps and inside the manor house. As Joshua looked around, he could see his men dead on the ground and many of the staff. He knew all this would be bloody and personal till finally he heard a yell and looked to his left.

The Baron came out of the room and charged Joshua. The Baron had his massive hammer in his hands with blood all over it. He brought it down trying to strike Joshua, but to the Barons surprise the hammer hit Joshua's arm and stopped.

Joshua looked to the Baron. "Nice hit, you must be the Baron." Joshua said as he stepped to the side and punched the Baron.

The Baron went flying back into the den area which he came from and slammed into the wall. Even though Joshua was not very tall for some reason he took the full attack of the Baron and did not even move.

The Baron got up and looked at Joshua as his mask came off showing his face and the scars all over it. The Baron charged Joshua and shoulder hit him pushing him though the entry and into the other side of the manor and into the wall. But not though it as Joshua grabbed hold of the wall and stopped the Barons progress.

Joshua bought his hands down and axe hit the Baron right behind his head sending him down into the floor. Joshua dusted himself off looking down at the Baron. "Now why don't you just stay there. It will make things a lot easier." Joshua said.

The Baron shook his head and stood up looking at Joshua. Joshua just shook his head. "Ok have it your way. "Joshua said.

Joshua did not let the Baron attack and hit him with several martial strikes. The Baron had no time to react and feel back into the entry. Joshua keep up his attack the Baron could not do anything and was stunned what the hell was this small man. He had to be some type of creature but what was he. No one had ever matched the Baron with power or could hurt him, but this small man could do both.

For a moment the Baron was able to get some defense up for a moment but only for a moment as Joshua hit him into the fireplace causing it to collapse on top of him. The Baron was knocked out and Joshua stood there brushing himself off and looking down at the Baron. "Toughest fight I have ever had your reputation is well deserved Baron." Joshua stated.

Joshua looked over at three men. "okay dig him out." Joshua said.

Meanwhile upstairs man after man rushed up and keep firing cutting down more of the staff. But then as Joshua was coming out of the den area all the men feel back down the stairs as coming down the stairs clawing and biting every soldier was Mina and Lily, they were going nuts in a blood rage.

Joshua was not expecting both of them to be coming right at him and pulled two men in front of him just as they attacked. Both men yelled as a fist came out the back of each man with their hearts in the fists. Joshua took two steps back and he saw the two ladies.

"Not good, Not good at all" Joshua said to himself. He knew he could stand toe to toe with one but both ladies and if they were here that meant the Count was also close. He keep his eyes on every corner of the area looking for the Count as he was set to fight Mina and Lily.

Mina and Lily saw the three men uncovering the knocked out Baron. Lily screamed "I will Kill you all!"

Lily lost focus and charged the three men. All she saw was her husband down and she wanted blood for hurting him.

Joshua took a breath knowing all he had to worry about right at the moment was Mina. He charged her not letting her attack and put her back on her heels. But Mina was fast she was much more powerful than her daughter and she was able to catch Joshua's strike and twist him around and put him on his knees.

Joshua could not believe how fast Mina was and how strong she was. To him she was as strong as the Lady Carmella and then remembered Mina was Carmella's younger sister.

Mina pulled his head back and started to come down with her fangs. Her fangs were so close to Joshua's neck he could feel her breath on his neck. But just then Joshua remembered his device in his pocked. Joshua was not happy about using it. He always had some honor when fighting but this was life or death, and he had no choice. His hand went into his pocket on his thigh and pulled out a small black box and right as Mina was fixing to bit him, he struck her with it in the thigh.

The little box sent one thousand watts though Mina's whole body. Mina screamed loudly as whole body shook out of control and she feel back hitting the ground knocked out.

Joshua got up shaking his body and breathing hard looking down at Mina. "Dang your one hell of a vampire Lady Mina" Joshua said knowing exactly who Mina was. As Joshua recovered from the fight with Mina, he looked over to see how his men were doing in the next room.

Lily was in combat with the three men who were working on her husband. She rammed into all three of them. She grabbed the one on her left side and pulled him in and sank her fangs into his neck. She ripped his neck open and threw him into the wall as she spit out his flesh. "Eww cold blood your nothing but a ghoul" Lily said as she slammed the one in front of her into the groundbreaking the floor as she did. But the third one was able to dodge her and come up to her side just as Mina screamed.

Lily looked over at her mother taking her eyes off the third attacker and before she could react, he hit her with a device like the one Joshua had used on Mina sending ten thousand watts though Lily's body.

Joshua looked over as Lily feel to the ground near her husband. "Very nice work" Joshua said.

But as Joshua spoke a sword ran through the soldier standing and blood dripped from his mouth. The man feel in front of Joshua. To

Joshua surprise it was the Count and Velmar. The Count had his sword in his right hand and started to walk towards Joshua.

Joshua smiled "well well if it isn't the Count himself this is an honor" He said as he cracked his knuckles and started to walk towards the Count. The Count was totally focused on Joshua.

Velmar had gone over to check on both the Baron and Lady Lily. But as he got to them four men came down the stairs and attacked him. Velmar was a beast in combat as he went through the four men quickly and turned to look at Joshua.

As the Count got in range to attack Joshua, he heard a loud grunt and turned and to his shock he saw a sword run though Velmar from behind. As Velmar fell forward the Count saw Greggor standing there with his sword. Greggor picked up Velmar and through him out the window into the brush. Greggor then turned and looked to the Count. "Mother sends her regards Uncle" Greggor said to the Count.

The Count looked at Greggor and charged him with sword in hand. Greggor charged the Count and their blades clashed. Greggor was surprised by the power of the Counts swings but was able to match it. Both men bared their fangs as they keep fighting. Joshua watched the fight knowing not to get involved or Greggor would kill him. Greggor was on even par as they keep fighting.

The fight was now going thought the back of the house the Count keep forcing Greggor back through the house. Joshua had his men pick up the Baron, Mina and Lily and take them out of the house while Greggor and the Count fought.

The Counts rage was in full swing as he keep attacking Greggor all the way to the back of the house. But as they stepped out of the house Greggor rolled backwards off the back porch leaving the Count alone on the porch.

To the Counts surprise he was surrounded by Greggor's men. "Greggor stood up and then looked at the Count." Hit him now" Greggor ordered.

All of Greggor's men fired what looked like tasers at the Count and each one sent ten thousand watts into his body. The Count shook but did not go down and actually took a step towards Greggor.

"Hit him again" Greggor yelled. He knew he could not kill the Count, or his mother would kill him, but he had to drop the Count. A second round of tasers hit the Count and this time he feel to his knees and looked at Greggor. "You won't… win… Mary … is still…. Queen…" The Count said as he feel forward knocked out.

Out in the brush Velmar came to but blood was coming from his mouth. He saw everyone being taken out of the house. He put his hand on his vest and pressed a button inside his vest pocket. Velmar then feel back passing out at the moment the whole manor house exploded.

The explosion rocked everyone sending even Greggor and Joshua flying. The manor house was totally destroyed. Which blew up the elevator shaft that went to the catacombs down deep inside the mountain.

Greggor and Joshua got up. Greggor looked at the men around him. "Joshua get the rest of the men up and take that castle now!" Greggor yelled.

Greggor then looked back at the men who had the Count, the Baron, Mina, and Lily. "You men lets head back to the city with our captives, Joshua no mistakes got it." Greggor said to Joshua as he left with the prisoners.

As Greggor sat in the Vehicle looking over at the Count and Mina. He thought how easy it could be right now to kill them. But also knew his mother wanted them dearly. Greggor looked over at the driver.

"Let's hurry mother will be impatient if we are late and she will want her prizes" Greggor said.

# 13

# Attack on VonStine Castle

Joshua walked towards the Castle with the remainder of his men. He had lost more than he had expected at the Manor House. But now it was the big show, taking the Castle.

Joshua had his men spread out as they came closer to the Castle. But something was wrong. All the lights were off, and no counterattack from the troops in the Castle. Something was not right, and it made no sense. Joshua stopped, looked around, and then looked to his second.

"Fritz, take charge. I want that gate opened now!" Joshua ordered Fritz.

"Yes, Sir," Fritz replied.

Fritz and five men moved towards the Castle while Joshua watched. Joshua kept watching and thinking to him; this all was wrong. He and his men should be under heavy attack by now, but nothing was going on. Joshua kept watching. He knew something was going to happen. He had kept all of his men back but the ones that Fritz took. Joshua just new something was wrong for that reason he keep almost all of his men back to be sure.

Fritz and his men moved up to the gate, but still, no one in sight or any attack. Fritz and his men were right at the gate; no lights were on. Nothing made sense until one of Fritz's men found a note on the gate. Fritz's man opened the letter and looked at it. All it had on it was one word "BOOM!"

Along with the walls and the barracks above the gate, the Gate exploded in a massive fireball. Fritz and all his men were instantly killed. Joshua knew something like this would happen and now ordered his remaining men to rush the castle gate area. Joshua was trying to figure out who knew they were coming, for it had to have been set way before the attack even started.

The explosion shook the whole mountain, and Greggor looked back and up the mountain seeing the massive fireball. Greggor just shook his head as he looked over at the VonStine family. "I am impressed your men are fighting well. You should be proud even though they are all going to die. My hat is off to them." Greggor told the Count even though the Count was still unconscious.

The whole city of Teveahna shook from the explosion on the mountain. The people were all in their bunkers for safety and knew not to come out. But those who were visiting, and all the news media did not know about the bunkers, or anything set up per the Count's orders. As the reporters ran out of their hotel rooms, they were surrounded by men in black armored bodysuits and weapons.

"No one move," One soldier yelled.

A Lady with blond hair spoke up, "wait, wait, were reporters," she said nervously.

"The soldiers moved the group towards the courthouse area. They noticed a lovely blond-haired lady standing with soldiers around her in a red dress as they came to the steps. One of the soldiers went up to the steps and bowed to the blond-haired lady. The soldier then pointed to the reporters. The reporters could not hear what was said, but they saw the blond-haired lady smile at them.

Back at the VonStine castle, Joshua's men were rushing through the rubble of the gate to get into the central yard of the Castle. But as they came in, machinegun fire rained down on them from four points. The guards who had stayed behind were now executing their plan. They had set up machinegun nests from four points and would remain there till they ran out of bullets.

The bullets shred Joshua's men one after the other. They were pinned down and tried to return fire, but it was no use. Joshua was impressed, but still, where were all the men at. The guards numbered one hundred. This all seemed wrong in Joshua's thoughts.

The machineguns finally ran silent, and Joshua's men finally advanced into the yard. Again, no guards were seen. Joshua's men rushed into the garage area and the main keep area of the Castle. Joshua sat down on the rubble, looking at the Castle. The men started to search around everywhere, looking for people.

A group of twenty men moved into the garage area. They found the Queen's beloved Integra and the Rolls Royce as they came into the Garage. The men still did not see anyone inside the Garage, but they were being watched.

From the safety of the VonStine Keep at the lake, Oscar was watching closely on his monitor pad. Morgan looked over Oscar's shoulder.

"Oscar, how are things going?" Morgan asked.

Oscar looked over his shoulder. "There are men in the Garage. Want me to blow it up with them in it. Our men have moved to the main hall for the last stand. I can blow it and take out about a third of all the men attacking. "Oscar said to Morgan.

Morgan looked at the monitor and smiled "Do it" I want to kill all those monstrous bastards. "Morgan said.

Oscar just smiled and touched his screen. When his finger touched the screen, little red lights in the Garage flicked. All the men who were under Joshua's command saw them. They panicked and tried to run out of the Garage, but it was too late as the bombs went off with several connected to the Castle's fuel depo at the back of the Garage.

The explosion rocked the whole mountainside and sent men flying everywhere. Joshua was also hit even though he was sitting on the rubble at the gate. The blast was so powerful it knocked Joshua over and even burned him slightly. Joshua stood up, dusted himself off, and saw the Garage blown away with car parts everywhere.

Joshua ran his hand through his hair and sighed. "Man, these guys are really starting to piss me off," Joshua said to himself.

At that moment, the rest of the men got up and attacked the front doors. The guards were all set for the last stand inside the main hall. The Captain of the Guard came out to join them from the back. The men were shocked. They were sure the Captain had gone with the rest of the people.

"I am Captain of the Guard of this Castle, and I will stand till the last. I know the First Knight will lead and win this war. But I will fight beside you men. We have served the Count and our Queen as best we could. Our families and children know what to do. I have no regrets, and it's been an honor serving with you men." The Captain said to his men.

Morgan and Oscar were watching and could hear what the Captain had said. "That old man, I knew he was going to do that. Let's make sure not to disappoint him in this war. "Morgan said to Oscar.

Oscar just nodded in response as they watched the inside of the Castle. They could hear the main doors getting banged on and watched as the small group of guards was ready to fight. Oscar looked at Morgan for the signal to blow up the Castle. Morgan glanced at Oscar as he watched.

"When the Captain falls, blow it up," Morgan said with a whisper.

Oscar just nodded and watched. As the doors fell and the men rushed into the Castle, they were met by machine gunfire. But this time, it was not as big a blood bath as the first. Joshua's men through several grenades and the guards pulled back. One by one the guards fail. But the guards keep fighting as they pulled back. Till finally at the main stairs, only one was left. The Captain himself. The Captain was hit several times but kept getting back up. Finally, the Captain looked up at one of the miniature cameras, smiled, and fell backward.

Oscar knew that was the signal. Morgan tapped Oscar on the shoulder. "Do it" was all Morgan said. Oscar taped his monitor screen. "Goodbye, Captain," Oscar whispered.

Joshua was standing on the steps as he felt the ground shake. He looked down and remembered that the wine seller was below him, and all he could say was "Oh .. Shi....." was all he got out of his mouth as it seemed the whole face of the mountain blew up.

The massive explosion sent debris all over the city down below. The massive explosion could be seen as far north as southern Germany and as far south as Italy as it lit up the night sky.

The Prime Minister and his staff at the military base could see it as every soldier just looked on in shock. The aid to the Prime Minister came up beside him.

"Prime Minister, what shall we do. That had to have been VonStine Castle. "The aid said to the Prime Minister.

The Prime Minister just looked down to the ground and started to cry. His country was being destroyed, and he was powerless to stop them. "I don't know" was all he said.

As the Prime Minister stood crying, his cell phone went off. The Prime Minister took his phone and looked at it. His eyes went wide as he saw the name on the phone who was calling. The Prime Minster fumbled with his phone before answering it.

"Your Majesty, are you alright? Where are you?" The Prime Minister asked as everyone gathered around. "Yes, your Majesty, I under, wait, what do you mean you have an army. What army?" The Prime Minister asked again. "Your Majesty, something terrible has happened to the city of Teveahna. All we know is a massive explosion that we could see. We think it was the Castle, but we have no word on anyone up there. All our aircraft are damaged, and the pass has collapsed to cut off the city. It will take days to clear it. "The Prime Minister explained to Mary.

Mary looked over at everyone with tears in her eyes. "They have attacked Teveahna, and most likely, the Castle has fallen. "Mary told everyone.

Mary asked. "Were any aircraft not on base during the attack."

The Prime Minister looked over at the General. "Do we have any aircraft that were not on base?" The Prime Minister asked.

The General looked to his men for answers. The soldiers scrambled to find out. A short time later, several soldiers ran up to report. They had found out that eight super cobra gunships were in Germany and scheduled to come home in a few hours. They had been in Germany for joint training.

Mary looked over at everyone and gave them the information. Albert started pacing back and forth, coming up with a plan. As Albert kept walking, Mary's cell phone went off. It was Sherriff Phillips.

Mary answered the phone "Hello,"

Mary was relieved it was David on the phone. "Oh, thank God you're all okay," she said.

Mary listened for a moment, then sighed" I see. So, the Castle is gone, and the Manor house as well. No word on the family. Okay, and what do you have at the keep? Alright, let me talk to my First Knight." Mary said as he walked back and forth.

"I see, and who sent you? My Grandmother, and precisely who is my Grandmother? Describe her to me. Alright, I believe you. So, what is your plan?" Mary asked.

"I have an army here where I am, and we are on the way. Don't do anything till I get there. Oh, and one last thing, eight super cobra gunships are coming back from Germany." Mary said.

"I can do that. We will talk soon, my Knight," Mary said as she closed the phone call.

Morgan looked over at David and handed him his phone back. "Well, at least the Queen is safe. She is sending us some cobra gunships to help out. They should be here in about two hours." Morgan said.

"She also said not to move till she got here," Morgan said.

Everyone looked around at each other and wondered how the Queen would get to them in such a short time. Morgan started to think of a plan now that he knew what he had to work with, as in men and equipment.

The VonStine Castle lay in ruins on the mountain with only rubble now and fire. But from the wreckage, a burned hand raised up, and slowly a man stood up; his body was burned badly but was starting to heal as he walked out of the rubble. As his body began to recover, it was clear it was Joshua.

Joshua looked around and shook his head. "Dam it, I knew it was off, but man, I could not have dreamed they would blow up the whole side of the mountain. I know one thing. I will kill everyone before I am done. "Joshua said as he started to walk down the mountain.

As Joshua walked down the mountain, he looked around at what was left of the castle and manor house and then counted. Eighty five guards were missing, so where did they go. Something was way off, and Joshua still could not figure out what was going on. How could that many men vanish so fast and not just that where were they all at.

# 14

# Carmella and the press

The blast of the explosion rocked the City of Teveahna. Every building in the city shook, and some had their windows blown out. The
reporters huddled together as the blond-haired lady turned and looked
up at the mountain and then looked down the steps seeing the armored vehicles pull up. As guards ran down and opened the side sliding
doors. Greggor got out and started walking up the steps to his mother.

Carmella looked down seeing Greggor coming up with the prisoners.

"I wanted prisoners, not a mountain blown up. You have some explaining to do, my son. "the blond-haired lady said.

Greggor walked up and kneeled in front of his mother. "I am sorry,
mother, they had set up a trap for the men. Though we did capture the
Count, Baron, Lady Lily, and the Lady Mina, no one else survived the
attack." Greggor said.

The lady with blond hair turned to look at the reporters. "The only
reason you are all alive is you are reporters. So, let's get down to business, shall we? Who are the ones who work cameras." She asked.

Two men raised their hands, and several soldiers came up and took
them away to get their cameras. The reporters remaining were a man
and a woman. The man looked in his early forties with short black hair
and was clean-shaven. He was in a black jacket and slacks. The woman
was in sweats as she had just come out of her bed and did not change.
She had short brown hair and looked to be around thirty-five years old.

Greggor had his men start building something in the square, and to his surprise, he saw Joshua walking into the city square. Joshua's body was almost fully healed. Not even a scar could be visible.

Greggor motioned his men to get Joshua some clothes as he laughed. "Well, look what walked in. I take it the blast was a surprise to you, and how many men did we lose? "Greggor asked.

Joshua looked at Greggor and smirked "Everyone is dead, and no way anyone lived through that blast. "Joshua replied.

Greggor crossed his arms "You did," Greggor said to Joshua.

Joshua just shook his head and put on the clothes he was given. Just then, the soldiers returned with the cameramen. The blond-haired lady was finally ready to talk.

"Are you all set up now? "Greggor asked the reporters.

The male reporter looked to Greggor. "Yes, sir, we're all ready to go," he replied.

The blond-haired lady stood in front of the reporters as the cameras started to roll. A soldier ran up to the Prime Minister and his officers in the capital.

"Sir, there is a live report coming from the city of Teveahna," The soldier said.

The Prime Minister and his officers ran over to a television to watch what was going on in Teveahna. To their shock, none other than Carmella herself was on screen.

"Oh no, Carmella," The Prime Minister said.

Carmella stood in her red dress, and all her men were around, with her son Greggor standing to her side. The male reporter turned and looked at the cameras and waited to talk. The lady reporter gave him the signal to start as she stood by the cameramen.

"We interrupt your scheduled programming for this emergency broadcast; This is not a drill. We are coming to you live from the old capital of Boldovia, the city of Teveahna. As you can see, it has been taken over by an unknown force." The man said while the cameras panned over the city. Showing the destruction on the mountain and what was left of the VonStine castle.

"As you can see, the city has fallen, and the VonStine castle is now in ruins." The reporter said.

"This lady here is the leader and wishes to make a statement." The reporter said as he finally turned and faced Carmella. "Would you please introduce yourself and give us your demands." The reporter asked.

Carmella smiled "I am the Duchess Carmella Diana Valmor of Boldovia," the blond-haired lady dressed in red said.

"This man beside me is my son Greggor," she added.

"Now, let me tell you a story. You have all heard the history story of the Great Prince and his gallant stand that took his life. We all know that story and his younger brother, who died soon after. But no one knows who he was or his name. There are no records of his name, nowhere at all." Carmella stated.

The reporter looked at Carmella. "That is correct. No one knows who his brother was." the reporter said.

Carmella continued. "Do you want to know why? Of course, you do; I know you do. Well, here is the truth. On that day of the battle, The great prince's brother did fall. But he did not die. He has never died. In fact, he is right over there." Carmella said as she pointed to the Count as he was being raised up on a cross.

"That is right. That man right there is, in fact, is Count Valdisoph Vicious VonKomfoang, the younger brother of the Great Prince. But his real name is actually Prince Valdisoph VonStine! He did not die on that day. Oh no, he, like his wife, the lady Mina Elizabeth Anette Valmor, who is right beside him." Carmella yelled as Mina was raised on a cross. Lily and the Baron would also join them on crosses.

The reporter was speechless, as was everyone watching in Boldovia. Carmella was blowing the door wide open. But the female reporter looked confused and asked. "How that happened right at five hundred years ago. How can someone be alive, let alone his family?" she asked.

Carmella motioned the female reporter to come over to her. "Come here, and I will tell you how," Carmella told the reporter.

The female reporter walked over to Carmella, and as she got close to Carmella. Carmella walked right up to her. "you want to know how they have stayed alive for five hundred years. It's easy, my dear. We are all Vampires," Carmella said as she grabbed the lady's hair, pulled her head back, and sank her teeth into the lady's neck right in front of the other reporter and cameramen. Carmella drank the lady dry and just dropped the husk of her body on the ground, looking at the cameras.

"This is the dark secret of Boldovia. It's full of monsters. And the family, the Royal Family, are all monsters. "Carmella proclaimed.

The male reporter and cameramen were all shaking, looking at Carmella.

"But what of the Boldovian Queen?" The reporter asked.

"Oh no, bother, my other son has already killed her. The Royal family is no more. And when those four there die, this country dies." Carmella stated.

As Carmella talked with the press, Joshua looked around and then looked at Greggor. "Something is not, right?" Joshua said.

Greggor looked at Joshua. "What do you mean we have the Count, Baron, Lily, and Mina? The Queen is dead. We have won."

Joshua shook his head. "Look around. Do you see any people? Where are the firefighters? The City Hall is on fire. The Castle and Manor are on fire and in ruins. But still no police, no fire, no people. This doesn't seem right." Joshua said to Greggor.

Greggor looked around and then noticed the lights around the square were all out. "Get the men ready for battle and set up the defensive area's around the city. Do it now. "Greggor ordered.

Joshua called over the commanders. "This is looking like a trap. Get the men ready for battle and set up defensive measures on all roads leading into the city. Get to it now. We may be attacked at any moment." Joshua commanded.

The commanders ran off to get their troops in place and make sure nothing could sneak up on them and attack them. Soldiers were running all over the place as Carmella looked over at Greggor.

"What is going on, Greggor," Carmella asked her son.

Greggor kneeled before his mother. "It seems we may be in a trap as no one has come out for the fires or even given resistance to our invasion," Greggor told his mother.

Carmella looked around and saw what was going on and grew angry. She stormed over to where the Count was. She looked at the Count, then at her sister Mina.

"What have you done? Where are all the people!" Carmella yelled at the Count.

Mina looked down at her sister. "Why are you doing this, sister?" Mina asked.

"Why? Why, dear, sister? You know why. Or should I remind you? Your beloved Count and his brother, the Great Prince, promised to protect our family remember. It was supposed to be me who married him, but you stole his heart and left the family to be butchered and me raped repeatedly by the invaders back then. The Prince promised to come and protect us. But did he? Hell no, he abandoned us, and you know it." Carmella screamed at her sister.

"You're wrong, Carmella. We did sent soldiers with a message to your father to bring everyone to the Castle. But he refused and stated he would defend his keep no matter what. Your father doomed you, not Me, nor my brother." The Count replied.

"You lie. You got my sister and left us to die. I swore revenge, and I almost have it. That dam werewolf I sent to attack your daughter and her husband failed back then. But this time, I have you all. Oh, and that Queen of yours. Oh yes, I know all about her. But it matters not. She is dead. And when the sun comes up, you are all dead. "Carmella screamed as she walked back up the steps in front of the main doors of the courthouse.

Deep under the Cathedral in the catacombs, Police Chief Ludwig was with his men. They had planned this out, so they all had weapons and tactical gear. Everything had gone exactly as the Count had planned so many years ago. His men had given him reports of what was going on. The destruction of the Police station at the courthouse and information about where men were placed throughout the city . The

THE STINES III: BATTLE OF TEVEAHNA

Castle and the Manor house, the Count, Baron, Mina, and Lily were captured.

Chief Ludwig was looking over a map of the city as his men kept giving reports. Finally, he saw something interesting and called for his deputy. The deputy came over. "Yes, Chief, what is it?" He asked

"Look on the map. This river runs and splits in half and wraps around the middle of town. But not just that, look here at the marks on the map. Those are explosive marks. Take two men and go see if those are explosives and if so, they should be in some tunnels." The Chief ordered.

The deputy took two men and went off down the catacombs to check and see what they could find.

The Mayor sat quietly listening to what was going on, and then noticed the Chiefs phone.

"Chief, is your phone satellite or cellular?" The Mayor asked.

The Chief looked at his phone for a moment, then at the Mayor. "It's satellite. Why do you ask?" The Chief replied.

"Great, that means it is secure, and outsiders trace cant. you can call Albert and see if the Queen is okay." The Mayor said.

Back in Monte Carlo at the court of the Wolf King, Albert's phone went off. Albert quickly pulled it out and answered it.

"Hello," Albert said.

"Oh, father, thank God you're okay. "Albert replied.

Mary walked over to Albert's side to listen.

"We are in the Catacombs just as the Count told us to do many years ago. We are ready to fight. But they have us outnumbered. Is the Queen alright, Albert" The Chief's voice asked.

"Yes, I am fine, Chief Ludwig," Mary said.

"Good to hear. I have two hundred and fifty men ready to fight. But It looks like Carmella has around seven hundred. I am sorry, my Queen, your Castle is destroyed." The Chief. said.

"Chief Ludwig, I am going to text you a number. That number is for David Phillips, the friend of my father, the Sherriff. He is at the lake fortress with my royal guard. They all made it out alive. My first knight is planning a counterattack. Get in touch with him and work things out. But do not move till I arrive with the army here." Mary said.

"Wait, you have an army? What army and how many men?" Chief Ludwig asked.

"We have five hundred werewolves coming with us. But don't do anything till we get home. Also, keep everyone hidden till the time to attack, no heroics." Mary said.

"Understood, my Queen," Chief Ludwig said as he hung up the phone and waited for the number. Mary looked to Albert as he texted the number off her phone.

The Chief called the number Albert sent. "Hello, this is Chief Ludwig," He said.

"Hello, Chief. Good to hear your voice again. One second will pass the phone to the First Knight. He is in charge." David said as he gave Morgan the phone.

"Hello," Morgan said.

"Hello, I am Chief Ludwig. The Queen gave me this number. We are in the catacombs under the Cathedral in the city's heart. "Chief Ludwig said.

"Good, very good; how many men do you have, Chief," Morgan asked.

"I have two hundred and fifty. We are armed and in battle armor, ready to go but the Queen said wait till she arrived and would give us a signal to look for." Chief Ludwig told Morgan.

"Yes, I got the same message not to move till then. Can you give me any information about what is going on in the city?" Morgan asked.

"Right now, we are checking the catacombs, but it looks like an underground river splits and runs around the city's heart. Not only that, but it seems explosives were set back during the war with Germany. So, we may be able to blow that and cut the heart off from the rest of the city." The Chief said.

"Also, from what we can gather, Camella is in front of city hall with about one hundred men. The rest of her men, which we think are around six hundred, are spread out on the main roads expecting an attack. Oh, and one last thing. They have the Count, Baron, lady Mina, and lady Lily." the Chief said.

"Understood, I will work on an attack plan, so stay put and don't do anything stupid for now. "Morgan said as he hung up the phone.

Morgan looked at everyone and then at the map. "Okay, see if you can find me a map to the catacombs. It seems we have a river running through town," Morgan said.

David walked over to Morgan. "What are you planning on doing?" David asked.

Morgan looked at David. "How much do you know about what is going on. I mean, what is really going on?" Morgan asked.

"What do you mean?" David replied

"You understand that this whole thing started five hundred years ago. Do you know why the Queen's parents were really killed? And why Carmella is hell-bent on killing everyone." Morgan said.

David, Crystal, and the Judge were all taken back.

"What do you mean? It was a hit squad to take out the ruling family of Boldovia, wasn't it." David said.

Morgan looked to Oscar. "Oscar, give them the history lesson while I work on the battle plan," Morgan said.

Oscar came over to the group. "Yes, boss."

"Five Hundred years ago, the battle everyone talks about took place, and The Great Prince as he is known did die. What was kept secret is that his younger brother, who there is no written name down for him in the history books, did not really die in that battle. You see, the younger brother made a deal with the ancient God Anubis and became a vampire. You met the Count, the man who walked Queen Mary down the aisle at her wedding. That was him, the Vampire Count. Since then, he has saved the country and has been its protector, and Lady Mina is his wife. She is also a Vampire. The VonStine family are all monsters in some way or fashion.

Now, as for what happened in the United States. Victor, Mary's father, was not a monster but was the direct decadent to the throne. But Mary's mother Isis, now that's different." Oscar said.

Everyone was shocked at what they were hearing. But Crystal especially was shocked about Isis. "Wait, I have known Isis since I was a teenager. She was no monster." Crystal said ecstatically.

"I never said she was a monster, but she was not human either. You see, Isis was an Egyptian Godling. That is why she was so beautiful, why the Queen is so beautiful, and why everyone flocks around her.

The VH corporation, known as the Van Helsing Corporation, is set up to hunt and eradicate Monsters and unique beings. They are the ones that came that night and killed Victor and Isis. They did not get Mary because her records had been hidden, and no one knew about her."

Mary, along with the Count and some other special people, brought down the VH corporation enough that the vampire Carmella took it over. She was the one behind its downfall and the house of Lee.

Carmella is the older sister to the lady Mina, wife of the Count. She wants revenge on the VonStines and has done everything to destroy them. But like the VH corporation, she did not know about Mary till after she took the throne. This is her last gasp, and she has her army, and that is what has control over the town. "Oscar said

"Then what exactly is Mary?" The Judge asked.

"She is the Queen of Boldovia, Daughter of Victor and Isis VonStine, and Granddaughter of the Gods Anubis, Bastet, and Sek-Met. She is a Demi-god like those of the Greek stories. "Morgan said to everyone.

"You mean like Heracles and the others," The Judge said.

Morgan just nodded. "Yes."

The Judge looked at Crystal and David. "You know it does make sense. After all, Mary never got sick, nor did the weather ever affect her. Wait, then Victor always knew as well. That sneaky little." The Judge said.

David smirked. "I wish Victor were here. He would be lets go and losing is not an option. But something is bothering me. How do you two know all this? "David said as he looked at Morgan and Oscar.

Oscar looked to Morgan before Morgan moved away from the table and looked at everyone.

"That's because Oscar and I used to work for the VH corporation as their top monster hunter team. This is our last mission, a mission to set everything right. I was the one who leaked all the information to Mary to take the company down. Mary is the key to everything. A world where we all can live together. No more hunting and killing people because we see them as monsters." Morgan said.

"Tell me how you become Mary's First Knight if you're the greatest monster hunter around Sir Morgan," David asked.

"Because Sek-Met asked me to. And saying no to an Egyptian cat goddess is not a good idea." Morgan said, handing David the letter to read.

"That letter is for the Queen from her Grand Mother Sek-Met." read it for yourself, and you will see why I am here," Morgan said.

David handed the letter back to Morgan. "I believe you, but now we have to finish this. It's what Victor would want." David said.

David let Morgan get back to work as he walked over to Crystal and the Judge. "That's a lot to take in. But if this is all true then that means Victor knew all this way back when we were in the Army together. I still remember when I first met Isis. Victor said he met her while he visited family in Europe. I bet he had met her when he was visiting in Egypt just after the war. He took two weeks sand visited Egypt and then he went to Europe, and we meet in Germany to come home. A few weeks later Isis showed up and Victor. That's right Victor went to the airport to pick her up. So, he always knew, and he keep it quiet." David said quietly as he remembered.

The Judge looked at David. "If this is all true what else is true? How many more people are like Mary that are out there and if Sek-Met is real how much more from ancient times are truly real and myth?" The Judge said questioning things.

"It's just shocking none of us ever noticed anything for all this time." Crystal said.

"Yes, I know it was strange that Victor had that book and phone number hidden and locked away like he did. It makes total since now that we think about it. Everything Victor did makes since now and how protected Mary was. It all fits. "David said.

But now all they could do was wait and Morgan keep working on a plan of attack. What was Mary planning on doing and how was she going to get here with her army.

# 15

# The Veil Falls

Monte Carlo Mary, along with her group and the King of the werewolves and his army, all awaited on the beach area for Hades and Persephone to arrive. King Zagreus was pacing along the beach area. His rage was overflowing. He wanted vengeance on the Vampires who attacked his people and killed one of his sons.

It would not be long as Hades and Persephone arrived out of a cloud of smoke. But unlike last time, Hades had his black hair in a ponytail and was in a black suit with a black tie and walking cane. Persephone was in a lovely short black dress and thigh-high boots. Her black hair was also in a ponytail.

Hades walked up to everyone. "Zagreus, are all your men ready? My minions have seen that Carmela has taken the city, but it seems the city was more of a trap for her as if they were expecting her. Child of Anubis, would you know anything about this?" Hades asked Mary.

Mary was stunned for a moment. "No one has ever called me that before, But we did talk with Albert's father and my First Knight to get a rundown on what is going on in Teveahna. The Count had a plan in place that everyone would go to the catacombs he built below the city if Carmella did take the city. It was tied into an underground river that ran around the heart of the city." Mary said.

Hades smiled. "An underground river, you say. How interesting." Hades started to have a plan. He took out a bag from his side and counted what was inside it as he looked at everyone. Persephone walked up next to her husband. "Dear, what are you up to?" she asked.

Hades looked to his wife and smiled" getting them to Boldovia though it's not going to be cheap." He said.

Everyone wondered what Hades was up to, but it did not take long to find out. Hades motioned everyone to follow him as he struck his staff into the beach four times. Near the beach was a small rocky hill, and at the face, a cave opened up.

Hades started to walk toward it with everyone following behind him. As everyone entered the cave, it turned out to be a tunnel going down with strange statues holding torches for light. Mary and Albert's armors automatically pulled their helmets up, which allowed them to see just fine. Hades kept walking further down in the tunnel till it opened up into a cavern, and everyone could see a river and waiting there was a large ferry waiting at the bank of the river.

As everyone made it to the riverbank, a cloaked figure came to the edge of the Ferry and looked down. The person's face was hidden from everyone, but Hades knew who it was.

"Greetings, Charon. I require your services." Hades said.

The cloaked figure looked down at the group. "Greetings, Lord Hades. What do you request of me?" Charon said.

"I request travel for all those who stand with me," Hades told Charon.

"I cannot, Lord Hades. They are not passed on and still breath?" Charon stated.

"Charon, I am requesting these taken to the lands of the Vampires, not to the underworld," Hades said.

"Ah, you know the price. Are you prepared to pay for the travel?" Charon told everyone.

Hades looked at everyone, then walked up to Charon and dropped the bag he held into Charon's palms. Charon counted the coins and then looked to Hades.

"You are short two coins. That one there cannot go, for she holds another in her." Charon said, pointing to Tasha.

Everyone looked at Tasha, and Edward walked over to her. Edward took her hand and smiled.

"You haven't said anything. Why did you not speak up.?" Edward asked Tasha.

"I didn't know I had only been sick for a few days in the mornings. Nothing else." Tasha said

Mary walked over to Charon and looked at the cloaked figure. She opened a small pouch on her belt, took out two coins, and handed them to Charon.

"Will this cover the shortfall for her to come?" Mary asked.

Charon took the coins and put them in the bag. The Charon motioned everyone to come onto the Ferry. Charon then looked to Mary again.

"It has been a very long time since I last saw one like you step onto my Ferry. It is good to see those young are still around." Charon told Mary. Mary just smiled as she got on the Ferry.

Hades and Persephone joined everyone as the Ferry pulled away from the shoreline. Charon would steer the Ferry along the riverway. The river would run through a massive tunnel system where stone statues stood on both sides with torches lighting the way. The tunnel was smooth black limestone or looked like that. From the ceiling, stalactites hung down.

Mary looked to Albert. "I never dreamed this was real. The afterlife is so much more complicated than I ever dreamed it would be." Mary said.

Albert just nodded as the Ferry kept on its path. The werewolf army was getting ready. They were checking all their weapons. They had an extensive array of weapons, from several miniguns to swords and axes. They had it all. Others were making sure body armor was right. Many of them had already shifted into their war forms for their armor to fit correctly.

Carmella knew they had about ten more hours till the sun would come up, and she would watch her sister and her family all burn alive. She only had to hold out till then. But something was troubling her.

She had not heard from her son Demitriof for some time, and no one could get him or any of his men on the phones.

Greggor walked over to his mother and looked down at her. "Mother, is everything alright?" He asked.

Carmella looked at her son. "No, I have not heard a word from your brother or any of his men. I am wondering if she managed to beat your brother and his men. Is she still alive? That is what has me troubled." Carmella said.

The cameramen and reporter caught this because they were filming all this live, and it was on all channels around the world. Now that everyone knew the truth and Vampires were real. Many governments were calling special sessions to talk about what to do. Germany, Austria, Switzerland, and Liechtenstein were in trouble for their governments always knew about the vampires and kept it secret now what they were going to do.

The Prime Minister had to keep Mary being alive a secret as best he could. But now, he was getting calls from countries worldwide wanting answers and if they needed to send troops to deal with these vampires. The Prime Minister reassured everyone who called they had things under control and would be dealing with them. If they needed help, they would contact everyone immediately.

As the Prime Minister sat down to watch the television and see what was going on in the city of Teveahna, he caught the part of Carmella saying she had not heard from her son and wondered if the Queen was still alive. He smiled, knowing that the Queen was alive and would do something. What that something was, he had no idea.

Back at the VonStine Keep, Morgan and the rest were around a large table with a map of the city. Morgan was making notes and trying to work out an attack plan. But he has very little tactical information on where all of Carmella's men were stationed. At the moment, all he could do was guess from what the police chief had told him on the phone.

While Morgan and the others were looking at the map, a guard came running in, yelling for a medic. Everyone rushed outside, and to everyone's surprise, Velmar, the Count's aid, and trusted friend staggered towards the keep.

Several guards ran up to him; one had a medical backpack, and they started to help Velmar. Morgan and David walked up along with some others. Oscar stayed at the table working on things. To Oscar's eyes, they did not have enough men. Even with all the police, they were still outnumbered two to one, which was terrible odds trying to take a city.

While the guards gave aid to Velmar, the ground near the lake shook wildly like an earthquake was taking place. A large Ferry rose out of the lake and came up to the shore, to everyone's surprise. The plank lowered from the side of the Ferry with Mary in her full armor coming down the walkway. Behind her were Albert and everyone else, along with the King of Werewolves and his whole army of werewolves.

As this took place, Oscar rushed out of the keep to see what was going on and just stood there with his mouth hanging open. Morgan could not believe what he was seeing. But before he could say anything. David, Crystal, and Judge Lepedrum were all hugging Mary.

Morgan coughed to get everyone's attention "As much as I love this reunion, and I really do, we have work to do and a battle to win." Morgan told everyone.

Mary looked at Morgan and Oscar and walked up to them. "I take it your, my First Knight. I also believe you have something for me," she said. Morgan gave Mary the note from Sek-Met. Mary took the letter and opened it.

"Mary, this is all we can do to help you. The man you see before you is Jay Lester Morgan. I have sent him to you as your First Knight. He knows more about Carmella than anyone except for the Count. Listen to him, for he will be able to beat Carmella. We love you and know you will win. But one last thing you need to know, Carmella is a Vampire, but her sire is not the Count. It is another that is as powerful as the Count and is, in fact, the first one to make a deal with your Grand Father Anubis. His name is Prince Vadisloff Dracul Tempest, and Carmella is one of his Brides. He has two others that are not as blood lusty as Carmella but still very dangerous, so watch out for them. love always Sek-Met."

Mary closed the letter and looked at Morgan. "So, my Knight, what have you come up with?" Mary asked.

# 16

# VonStine Keep

Charon and Hades, along with Persephone, left on the Ferry returning home to the underworld. But everyone knew that they would be watching.

Morgan escorted Mary to the large table inside the keep that had the battle map. Mary looked over everything as Albert, and the rest came in to see what Morgan had been working on.

"As you can see, your Majesty, this is all I can work up so far, I have no real intelligence on troop movement in the city, only what the Chief is calling me, and his view is limited," Morgan said.

John looked over to Rebecca. "Rebecca, take your pack and do a recon mission on the city. Make sure to keep out of sight. If possible, make contact with the Chief. But if not, don't risk anything. We will only get one try at this." John told his sister.

Rebecca nodded. "On it," she said as she left the room. Now they only could do was wait.

Rebecca walked out of the keep and got her pack around her to go over the plans. Rebecca made sure that everyone knew how important this mission was and that they could not mess it up. Every member understood as they all started to move out. They shifted into their wolf form and ran off into the night.

Oscar laughed to himself, watching the wolves vanish into the night. "Man, never thought I would be fighting on the side of the monsters, but this is what has to be done. "He thought.

Oscar came into the room, where everyone was looking over the map. He recognized John and the King, along with Albert and Mary. The rest he did not know. As he walked up beside Morgan, he kept looking at Albert's armor, and he tilted his head, studying it.

Albert looked at Oscar. "Something wrong," Albert said.

Oscar smiled. "Oh no, just your armor. It's not like any armor I have ever seen. Even the Queens is strange. What is it made out of, if you don't mind me asking? "Oscar replied.

Albert now understood. "Actually, I am not sure what they are made of. They were a gift from Mary's Grand Parents." Albert replied.

Oscar was shocked, as was Morgan, hearing what Albert had said. Morgan looked closely at both Albert and Mary's armor.

"So that is what mystical armor looks like?" Morgan said.

Everyone looked at both Albert and Mary for a moment. Mary shook her head. "Okay, Okay, yes, it's special armor. Now can we get back to business?" She said to everyone.

Just then, a guard came inside to let everyone know the super cobras had arrived and landed outside. Mary looked up, as did Morgan, as the pilots walked into the room. The pilots all bowed to the Queen and then looked to the rest. Morgan motioned them over to the map.

Rebecca and her pack had just made it to the fork in the road that split just outside of the city. Rebecca could see a checkpoint and that more men were backing it up with heavier fire power. The pack keep out of sight and moved around the checkpoint to go further into the city. The wolves split up and went looking and making mental notes of where Carmella's men were all spread out throughout the city.

Rebecca and two of her packmates made it to the Cathedral. From the back they went in and found Chief Ludwig and his men.

"Greetings Chief Ludwig I am Rebecca; John's sister were here with the Queen." Rebecca said as she looked at the Chief.

Chief Ludwig signed in relief. "Good to see you and great to hear the Queen is alive and well. What news do you have and how many soldiers did she bring with her?" Chief Ludwig asked.

Rebecca smiled. "The Queen brought five hundred werewolves and we are here to give these vampires what they deserve." Rebecca said.

The Chief would go over everything with Rebecca and how the city was all set up along with the catacombs and the river that ran under the city.

Rebecca thanked the Chief for the information and would relay all this information to Morgan the First Knight. But now she had to head back and meet up with her pack so they could get all this information back to Morgan in time.

After about an hour the pack meet up and pulled out to return to the VonStine keep. Rebecca knew time was not on their side and they had to move quickly. Or all this would be for nothing.

Morgan again started to explain the plan when Rebecca walked in. "Were back," Rebecca announced as she joined everyone at the table.

Morgan was relieved to see Rebecca back.

"Were you able to make contact with the Chief and his men? What did you see?" Morgan asked.

Rebecca looked at the map. "We did make contact with the Chief. The whole downtown area is under Carmella's control. Not just that, but all electricity has been cut around the downtown area per the Count's plans. It seemed the Count had worked out a plan to keep the citizens safe if Carmella did attack." Rebecca said.

Morgan was shocked by this. But stayed quiet, listening to Rebecca's report, not wanting to interrupt her as she had the floor. Rebecca started to point out some things.

"We found that the pass is cut off caved in, so we are not getting any outside help. Second, where the rails meet with the road coming from the lake is heavily guarded with about fifty men and fortified so that it will be the first objective." Rebecca explained.

"Past that, they have hardened emplacements at every major crossing in town. Some of her men are up on top of the buildings in the downtown area. The Police station attacked to the city hall is on fire and in ruins." Rebecca said.

"I did see Carmella. She is with a large man and a smaller man and reporters at the top of the stairs going to city hall. But for some reason, the smaller man gave off a strange feeling of death. He may be a wild card and very dangerous." Rebecca told everyone.

"The Police are all under the Cathedral in downtown. They are all geared up and ready to fight. They just need to word, and they will come out and join us. The Chief said they have the underground river set to explode that can take out a major part of the downtown area, making it like an island for use to fight in. But again, they need some kind of signal to attack." Rebecca said.

Mary looked around, thinking, and then saw something on the wall and pointed at it. "What is that on the wall?" She asked.

Velmar looked over at the item on the wall and then at Mary.

"That is the royal battle standard, my Queen," Velmar told Mary.

"That's it, Rebecca, have one of your pack go back and tell Chief Ludwig to wait till he sees the battle standard flying on the downtown flagpole. At that moment, then come out fighting. "Mary said.

Rebecca nodded and left the room. Morgan looked over the map, pointing out a few things to the others in the room. Finally, he looked at everyone.

"We cannot mess this up. We are only getting one chance to fix all this. But remember, we have to rescue the royal family, kill all of Carmella's army and take back the city once and for all." Morgan told everyone.

Mary looked over at Tasha. "Tasha, you have to stay here. We cannot afford to lose you." Mary said.

Tasha was stunned. "Why, Hell no, I am going to fight. They killed my brothers. It's not fair. Mary, why?"

Mary walked over to Tasha. "Tasha, you carry the future of this kingdom. If we lose and I fall, you are the only one who can take the throne. Your baby is the most precious person in all the kingdom, and we can't lose you or the baby." Mary said.

Tasha had forgotten about being with child and now understood. "Your right, Mary, I forgot. I will stay here and stay safe." Tasha said.

Edward walked over and hugged his wife and kiss. "I will come back that I promise, and we will raise our child together. I Love you, Tasha." Edward told her.

As everyone left the room and headed out of the keep, Mary stopped. "I forgot Night Star," Mary said.

Albert turned to her. "No, no, Mary, don't do it. Let him be."Albert said franticly.

"But we need him. Trust me. I will be right back." Mary said as she ran off.

Albert just sighed as he turned and looked at everyone. Everyone looked at Albert, not understanding what just had happened and why Mary had runoff.

Morgan looked at Albert. "Okay, and who exactly is Night Star.?" Morgan asked.

Albert sighed again and very hesitantly said. "It's Mary's pet Dragon."

Everyone there said at the same time in a shocked voice. "HER DRAGON!"

Albert nodded. "Yes, she has a dragon." He said

Morgan just through his hands up and started to walk inside to get something to drink. "Sure, why not we have every other type of mystical creature here? Why not a dragon." He said.

Morgan looked at Albert. "Exactly how big is this Dragon, and what can it do," Morgan asked.

Albert replied. "well, it's big, you know, that television show a few years back with the girl who had the dragon. You know, in the last season, she road it and burned that army to the ground."

"You got to be kidding me. Are you telling me she has a Dragon that can breathe fire and fly that is big as that one in the show?" Morgan asked.

Albert nodded. "Yes, it's about the same size maybe a little larger"

Morgan just put his hand on his head and could not believe this.

"Oh great, this is not... wait a minute, I got an idea. Oh, this is going to work. I know exactly what we will do." Morgan said out loud.

Deep in the cavern, Mary had walked to the large doors that held her hidden treasury and the Dragon Night Star within. Mary opened the door and stepped inside. Mary walked inside and past her treasure and up to the lake that sat at the back. Flaming pits were all around to light up the cavern. Mary looked around.

"Night Star, are you here? I need your help." Mary said.

As Mary stood near the water's edge, the water began to move more and more, and it glowed red. Night Stars' massive head emerged from the water and rose above Mary several feet. Night Star looked down at the Queen. He was delighted to see her, but he had never seen the Queen in armor before.

"My Queen, it is always a delight to see you. But why are you in armor? Has something happened?" Night Star asked.

Mary nodded. "Yes, the evil vampire Carmella has attacked Boldovia. She has destroyed the castle and took the Count, Baron, my Aunts Lily, and Mina prisoner. She has also taken the town. I need your help to stop her and rescue the people of Boldovia and my family. Will you help me?" Mary asked Night Star.

Night Star came out of the water and looked down at his Queen. "Of course, my Queen, but will it not bring me out from hiding?" He said.

Mary looked at Night Star. "It doesn't matter now. The world knows about the family and the vampires. It's now out in the open. So, we have nothing left to lose. We now have to fight, win and rebuild." Mary said.

Night Star lowered his head so Mary could pet him as he thought for a moment. "My Queen, of course, I will aid you in your fight. I have lived only to protect the royal family, and you are Queen. I will destroy all who threaten this land, your people." Night Star said.

Mary was delighted, but then she remembered. "Night Star, how do we get out to join the others at the keep." She asked.

Night Star was surprised but remembered Mary had never seen him outside the cavern. "Oh, an underwater passage exits out in the lake. So, I come out of the water at night to hunt." Night Star said.

Night Star turned so Mary could climb on his back. Mary crawled up as her helmet activated, wrapping around her so she could see and breathe safely as they went into the water.

Everyone outside of the keep was shocked to see the massive dragon rise from the water and Mary on its back. Night Star flew over and landed in front of everyone and the Cobra gunships. Morgan watched as Mary got off of Night Star and walked over.

"Everyone, this is Night Star," Mary said, pointing to the dragon.

Morgan was shocked. He was joking about the size, but Night Star was that big.

"Well, now are we all here. Good time for plan B." Morgan said.

"This is how we are going to make our attack. John and Edward will be the spearhead of the army of Werewolves in a wedge formation. Inside the wedge will be the calvary. I will lead the Calvary. Oscar, you will carry the Queens Battle Standard. Make sure to raise it on the flagpole. David, you on my left, you will help in rescuing the family with back up by Rebecca's pack. Take their weapons so when they are free, they can fight. Third, Colonel take your Cobras to blow us a path to the center of town. Take out as many targets of opportunity as you can. And last but not least. Your Majesty. You and Albert will come in on Night Star and go directly at Carmella, They are yours, and Night Star say overhead pick targets you deem you can take out. "Morgan said, laying out the plan.

The King of the werewolves sat with Tasha as he listened to everything Morgan said. He looked over at Tasha and smiled.

"So, you finally did grow up. I am so proud of you. More than you could ever know, Tasha. You turned that wild wolf-boy into a loving husband and soon-to-be father. I wonder what the future holds for the rest of us, but at least you will be safe and happy. "The King told Tasha.

Tasha smiled and hugged him. "I Love you, Great Grandfather." She said.

Crystal walked up to her husband. David smiled at her and kissed her. "Don't worry, I will return, but I have to do this. Victor has to be avenged." David told Crystal.

Crystal tried to smile. "You better come back to me," she told David.

Judge Lepedrum walked up beside Crystal and looked at everyone. He just could not believe what he was seeing as he thought of Victor and all they had done in the past.

"All I have to say is give them hell," Judge Lepedrum said to everyone.

# 17

# The Rise of the First Knight

A Guard came over to Morgan as everyone was almost ready to head out for battle. The Guard told everyone that they had found the armor for the horses. Morgan told them to get the horses dressed for battle. This set things back for about an hour.

Morgan looked at everyone and then to Oscar, who was getting on his horse. A Guard handed Oscar the Battle Colors. Oscar looked over at Morgan. Oscar could see Morgan had a face of worry.

"You okay, Boss?" Oscar asked.

"Morgan looked at Oscar and nodded. "Ya, just this time were not sneaking in to hit and run. We are going into a real battle. Just I know not everyone is coming back on this one." Morgan said.

Oscar nodded to Morgan. "Yes, Boss, but we have to see this through, and you know, as I do, this is our last fight. One final ride, one final battle." Oscar said.

Morgan looked around again. The werewolves were all shifting forms and were in armor. Rebecca had not shifted just yet. She was going over everything with her pack and what their job was. Morgan took note of her and had a feeling he might have to help her in the battle. Maybe it was an omen or something, but who knows.

Morgan had one look at everyone and then looked to Mary as she and Albert were on top of Night Star. Mary stood up on Night Stars' head as he lifted her up.

"My Royal Guard, Those of the Werewolf nation. Tonight, we go into battle. Carmella has declared war on all of us. She wishes for all of us dead. This battle tonight is not just for me. It's not just for the people of Teveahna. Nor is it for Boldovia. This battle is for you and me and our loved ones. It's so they will have a home of safety and peace. Tonight, we fight to save those we love and get vengeance on those who attacked our innocent friends and family.

Remember, they will show no mercy to us. They will show no surrender, for we take no prisoners and fight till they are all dead or we are all dead. Now let's save everyone. "Mary said.

Everyone roared and cheered in agreement with what Mary had said. Morgan felt more at ease after hearing Mary talk. His heart was calm, and he prayed for the first time in a very long time.

"Great spirit of my people, I have not prayed in a very long time, and you may not hear me. But know this, I fight for what's right this night. I fight with honor for my people. I fight to save those who can't fight. If I fall this night, I fall a warrior of the Comanche, and I have no regrets. I ask you to watch over all of the warriors here, and I hope to make you proud of me one last time." Morgan whispered.

Morgan looked up at the moon, took his knife, and slit the palm of his left hand. He put his two middle fingers into the blood and marked his face with two lines down his cheek on his right side.

Night Star, at that moment, took to the air, followed by the eight Super Cobra gunships. Morgan looked at everyone.

"Let's move out," Morgan ordered.

John, Edward, and the pack took point with the werewolves in full armor, forming a V formation. The Calvary would be inside the V formation. Morgan was at the head of the Calvary with Oscar on his right side with the Queens Battle Standard. On his left was Sherriff David Phillips. A Sword for the count was on his back, and a mighty Hammer was on the horse's saddle.

They had to keep the horses quiet until they were almost in sight of the first set up fortification at the crossroads. The Super Cobras came in low while Night Star stayed up, watching the Cobras go in from the night sky. It was the first time Night Star had ever seen flying machines in the air.

As Night Star keep up in the clouds the Super Cobras stayed in formation and were just barely able to stay with the wolves and Calvary as they were so slow moving. But they were able to hover and then move forward.

The Colonel was in radio contact with Morgan and the Queen, as they keep moving forward.

"Alright Colonel light up the city pick any target of opportunity you find, and don't hold back." Morgan said on the radio.

"Yes sir. Good hunting. Alright lets rain hell on these Basterds" The Colonel replied with.

The Super Cobras let all hell loose on the fortifications, blowing it sky high. The explosions could be seen and heard in the city. Carmella and Greggor looked that way.

Joshua said, "I knew it, I knew it. Everyone prepare for battle for its coming, 'and we take no prisoners!" Joshua looked at Carmella for approval. Carmella nodded to Joshua and then motioned him to come to her.

"Yes, Mistress?" Joshua asked Carmella.

"Joshua, if things go bad, Kill the reporters," Carmella said.

Joshua just gave an evil grin. "Yes, Mistress," he said.

At the crossroads, John, Edward, and the pack hit the soldiers there that was still alive from the Cobra attack with other werewolves as backup. It was a blood bath as they ripped everyone to shreds. They knew that these men were vampires and not human anymore. So, the only way to defeat them was to kill them. John had gotten hold of one of the vampires, ripped his arms off, then clawed his throat out before taking his head off.

Edward saw one running and turned to see Morgan come up and cut him down with his katana. The Vampire burst into flames from the strike. Edward shifted down and looked at Morgan.

"What type of metal is that Katana made out of?" Edward asked Morgan.

Morgan smirked. "It's a blessed blade, a gift from Mary's Grandmother," Morgan said.

Edward laughed and shifted back to war form. But as he did more of Carmella's men arrived this fight was not over, and John and the wolves were ready. The clash was a hard fought battle as the Vampires were not caught off guard this time and they did not have support from the Cobras. Edward took several wolves and flanked the Vampires from the left. The Vampires tried to counter but Morgan and the Calvary were able to pin them down. Once all of the vampires in this area were dead Edward and the wolves with him joined John and the rest of the army as they were now on the city's outskirts. John looked at everyone, then at Morgan. "This is it, no turning back. Remember our objectives, and we leave no one alive on the other army. "Morgan said.

For now, the battle of Teveahna had begun. John, Edward and all the wolves split up into teams and moved out to clear the outer layers of the city. Morgan knew it was best at moment to hold up till they herd the wolves howl to attack.

# 18

# The Battle for
# Teveahna Begins

The lead Super Cobra came in low, and it's 20 mm Gatling cannon opened up on the next hardened fortifications. Metal and the Cars that blocked the roads were chewed up by shells hitting them. A second Cobra fired one of its Zuni rockets, slammed into the full blockade, and blowing it sky high.

Everyone at City Hall looked in the direction of the explosion and now saw the Cobras flying overhead.

Back in the Capital the Prime Minster and his Cabinet along with the General and soldiers all could see on the television the Cobra's attacking.

Cheers rang out all over the base as they saw the Cobra's open up on several hardened potions.

Carmella was livid as she screamed. "Where did those helicopters come from!"

Greggor had no clue he knew his men took out all the aircraft that Boldovia's Air Force had at the national base. Greggor looked to Joshua for an answer.

"I am sorry, Sir, no clue where they came from. I know they did not come from the bases here in the country." Joshua said

Greggor looked to the men at the base of the courthouse steps. "Get going and find out what is going on." He yelled at everyone.

Every man ran off to find out what was going on. But those in the square took places behind the fortifications they had made to protect the courthouse from attackers.

Just as several men got to the fortifications another Cobra came in from the opposite direction and fired two Zuni rockets into the hardened protection. The explosion lit up the whole square as vampires went flying in all directions. They were all on fire and trying to get their armor off. But it was no use as the Cobra opened up with its 20 mm Gatling cannon cutting the vampires down one after the other.

More of Carmella's men were able to make it past the burning mess that once as the fortified position. They broke up into units and started to look for attackers. They all knew that the Cobras were most likely not alone and that they had been told by Joshua about the lack of guards at the castle.

As the units moved down the street, they fanned out in groups of four. The teams split up and took different streets, heading to where the fork road area was. The first team arrived, and as they came around the last building, the first man was hit by 50 caliber rounds from a minigun. They were cutting him to pieces. Several others dropped down and opened fire blindly into the area.

The second, third, and fourth teams got to the spot simultaneously. To all their shock, it was not humans attack but werewolves and a lot of them. One member called for aid as he reported an army of werewolves. The werewolves saw the soldiers and turned to attack them. Every member started to fire their FAMAS rifle, trying to cut down as many werewolves as possible. The werewolves were wearing body armor, so many were not getting hurt. A few werewolves return fire, and at the size they were in their war forms, they could carry the 50 caliber miniguns solo with ammunition belts on their backs.

The werewolves moved out in groups of twenty with one heavy 50 caliber minigun in each group. John along with Edward and Rebecca along with their packs keep a vanguard in front of the Calvary as they keep moving down the main street towards the city center.

John motioned Edward and the pack to stay with him. As the werewolves got to a point where they could see Carmella and the Reporters John motioned Rebecca and her pack to break off and get to the reporters. The rest to spread out and pick targets to take out. They all knew they had to make a path for the Calvary to move through. The wolves keep moving through the lower outer part of the city. They were being hit by a massive counterattack from Carmella's men.

John's team went in further but all of a sudden, shots hit near them on the side of a building. John and his team were pinned now, and John had to think fast. He looked to Edward and motioned him to take three men with him, to head up the side of the building and come down on top of the troops shooting at them.

Edward slowly moved back into a darker area with three of the pack, and they slowly went up the wall of the building. It was only three stories, and they moved over the roof looking for targets and found five men behind a parked car. Edward motioned everyone to move in, and all four of them dropped from the roof on top of the five men.

Edward dropped right in front of all of them. His claws came across the first two men's midsections and sliced them open. Both men fell to the ground but were not dead. Edward's claws came down as they looked up, sliding down their faces and killing them. The other three werewolves hit the three soldiers, killing them all.

John and the rest of the pack came around to join Edward. The group kept moving on. The werewolves had to make a path for the Calvary, which was going slower than they thought. Morgan had held up the Calvary, not wanting to run into a massacre. Morgan looked at everyone. They all knew what was going on. Oscar looked to Morgan and then saw the Cobras fly over.

"You know they are seriously entrenched. "Oscar said.

Morgan nodded. "Yes, I know. The thing is, when the sun comes up, it's really going to be a mess. For my guess is they will kill the Count and the rest." Morgan replied.

David came up beside Morgan" Looks like things are going well, but urban combat is very tricky. This will take time. But the Cobras definitely help. "David said.

Morgan looked to David. "It's going too slow, but we can't risk it. We only get one shot at this. Wait a minute, your ex-army First Calvary if not mistaken." Morgan replied.

David nodded to Morgan. "Yes, but I was never part of the unit that had horses. I was with the Grey Wolves armored battalion. "David told Morgan.

Morgan smiled. "Good, so you know urban combat, I take it," Morgan asked.

David nodded. "Yes, that is why I liked your idea of sending the wolves in first and holding the Calvary. We can't make mistakes. We don't have the men to be sloppy." David said, looking at Morgan.

Joshua was looking around as the Cobras flew overhead. He had not gotten any information on what was attacking. He looked to Greggor and then ran down the steps and went into the city to see what was happening.

Foster had moved almost to the outskirts of town to where the gun-fire sounded. When he saw his men start to fall back, he yelled at them.

"Hold your ground! What the hell is going on!" Joshua screamed as he came up to his men. One soldier turned at looked at Joshua.

"Sir, It's werewolves and lots of them. They are in armor and have weapons. We are doing our best to hold them back, but we need more men. "The soldier said.

Joshua was looking at the soldier. "What do you mean werewolves? There should only have been about four or five at the moment at the Castle. How many can it ....." Joshua stopped talking when he saw several werewolves in armor come around the corner. Joshua pulled a short sword from one of his soldiers and turned toward the werewolves.

"Pull back. I will deal with them and get more men down here." Joshua yelled.

The men turned and ran off as Joshua started toward the were-wolves. The werewolves totaled twelve, and they saw Joshua as nothing.

Joshua is smaller than most, at only five foot six. But the werewolves found out fast that Joshua was more than he seemed.

Joshua ran headfirst into the werewolves and slid under the first one, slicing both thighs' inside as he did. Joshua stopped right in front of another one and stuck the wolf in the heart. Both were down and out of the fight. The other ten tried to get to Joshua. But due to his size, it made it hard for all ten to get at Joshua at once.

The wolves had to pull back some so not to hit each other. Joshua knew this would happen and used it to his advantage in the fight. He kept up his attack on the wolves closest to him. His blades kept slicing as the wolves missed with their claws, and no one had any weapons as this was a scout team.

Three of the wolves moved in against Joshua with claws and fangs. This time one tried to tackle Joshua, but Joshua side-stepped it and sliced down on the wolf's neck, killing it. As the other two tried to take Joshua down, Joshua was able to hit one of the two, but the third had him as the others moved in. The wolves ganged up on Joshua, clawing and biting him, but then the wolf holding him down caught up blood and let Joshua go. With the wolves on top of Joshua, they were easy targets for Joshua to slice and kill one after the other.

Just as Joshua was getting up and cleaning himself off from dirt, something caught the corner of his eye. He had seen the wolf pack of Rebecca trying to sneak into the city. They had their orders and were trying to stay out of fighting for now. But now Joshua saw them. He let out a smile and thought to himself. "Mmmm, more wolves to kill," and he ran off after them.

The soldiers Joshua had rescued ran to the train station, which was one of the locations where a massive number of soldiers were stationed. As they came in, all yelled. "Hurry, werewolves are attacking at the edge of town. Sir Joshua is their fighting and called for soldiers to come."

Soldiers left the train station heading to where Joshua had fought the wolves leaving a small group there. As the troops got to the location, they were met by a massive counterattack by werewolves. It was total mayhem as both armies slammed into each other. Claws, Swords, and bullets went flying all over. Wolf and Ghoul and minor Vampire all were in the mix.

One soldier had made it back to the square and the courthouse. The soldier ran up to Greggor and kneeled, panting. "My Lord, it's an army of Werewolves attacking." He told Greggor.

Greggor looked to his mother, Carmella, and then to the soldier. "How can this be? There are no werewolves but the few on the mountain. Where did they all come from? "Greggor demanded.

Carmella overheard all this and walked over to Greggor. "Have you had any contact with your brother?" She asked Greggor

Greggor turned and looked at his mother. "No, mother, I have not. You don't think?" he said

Carmella thought for a moment. She then remembered seeing Mary in some type of armor before the signal went out. Carmella turned and looked at the reporters and then at her son.

"Prepare to fight looks like your brother failed, and Mary is here with the werewolves. I don't know how she did it, but it looks like she did. "Carmella said.

Carmella wondered where exactly Mary was as she saw Greggor barking orders to men and watching the men run around all over. The reporters were trying to give updates as they saw the Cobras overhead attacking spots in town.

Back in the capital, the Prime Minister and staff were watching the television feed from Teveahna. They could tell something was going on, but they wondered how the Queen got there. Everyone was shocked at how she got there from Monte Carlo in just a few hours, but it looked like she was there with an army.

The Prime Minister looked to the General. "What news from the mountain pass? Do we know how long it will take to get it open, and what about the repairs on the helicopters?" He asked.

The General looked over at his men for reports. "Well?" was all he said.

"Yes, Sir, at the moment, we are looking at another two hours but should have two of the Chinook up and ready to fly. Our men will be geared and ready to go. As for the mountain pass, The destruction is terrible engineers say it will be at least two weeks before it is cleared to where we can run vehicles through." The soldier said.

The Prime Minister looked to the General. "Get the troops ready to go. I want them airborne as soon as possible." The Prime Minister said.

The Prime Minister walked back and forth as an aid brought him a cup of coffee. He looked up at the moon and prayed for this nightmare to come to an end soon.

As more men came from the central train station, two of the Cobra Helicopters locked in on the building coming in over the city square and let loose with their Hydra 70 rockets letting almost seventy-six rockets slam into the train station.

Carmella watched as the train station went up in a massive explosion. Soldiers went flying, many of them killed by the strikes. The Helicopters kept moving around, but they were having issues getting targets due to the streets and buildings.

The fire from what was left of the train station lit up the whole city square. Carmella shook her head and laughed and looked at her sister.

"Have to say Mary is making this fun. I can't wait to kill her in front of you."

The Baron had not said anything while being hung on the cross, but he was paying attention and looked at Carmella.

"You take Mary too lightly, Carmella. When they get here, you will have the fight of your life." The Baron said.

"Oh, look, the silent fool finally says something. Tell me how many hundreds of years you cared and oversaw the throne only to lose it to that girl. Hmm... tell me. I bet it burns you alive." Carmella said, taunting the Baron.

Greggor walked down to his mother and looked at those staked. His eyes fixed on the Count. "How did you know we would attack like this. I want to know exactly what tipped you off." Greggor yelled.

The Count looked down at Greggor. "Do you forget who sired your mother? He and I met long ago in a battle, and he used the same tactics, so it was easy to plan what you would do. I did have five hundred years after all." the Count said, teasing Greggor.

Greggor turned and stormed back up the stairs to the courthouse. It was luck or bad luck. You could say, depending on who it was. But Greggor looked up the steps just as Rebecca and her pack arrived to save the reporters.

"Oh, hell no!" Yelled Greggor as he pulled his sword and ran towards the reporters and the pack of werewolves.

Carmella turned and grew upset and went up the stairs with the sword her son had given her. "I am really getting mad. Kill them !" She screamed.

Rebecca saw Greggor and Carmella coming up the steps and then heard one of her pack let out a howl of pain. She turned around to see one of her pack fall from a knife strike from behind. To her shock, there stood Joshua.

"Finally caught up to you filthy animals," Joshua said.

Rebecca and her pack still outnumbered those around them, but she knew they were in major trouble and let out a massive howl to alert the rest they were at the reporters.

Morgan and the Calvary heard the howl. Morgan turned and looked at everyone. "Sound the Charge. It's time to attack." Morgan ordered.

The bugler sounded the charge, and Morgan and everyone headed for the square as the wolves came towards them from the sides as they rode to the square for a massive army and Calvary charge.

Greggor stopped his charge as he heard the bugle sound and looked to his left. "Get everyone back here now; the main force is coming. Prepare for an all-out battle. Joshua, kill the wolves. We will handle the charge." Greggor ordered.

From up in the night sky Mary was watching with Albert behind her on Night Star. Mary could see everything and saw the Calvary move in. She then moves up near Night Stars' ear. "Wait till you see the battle standard on the flagpole, then we dive on the blond lady at that building. "She said as she pointed to Carmella.

The Cobras regrouped and came in to give aid to the Calvary, shooting down any hardened areas that were still in the way. Morgan looked up at the Cobras overhead and smiled as they kept moving in. Morgan was surprised the Cobras had destroyed the train station. But he knew something bigger was fixing to happen.

# 19

# The Battle of Teveahna Square

Morgan was at the lead of the Calvary charge, but just before they made it to the city square, John and Edward and their pack came around to take the lead. They knew Rebecca was in trouble as they advanced, and they had to act fast.

Carmella with Greggor moved to the front of city hall. Carmella looked over at Joshua, who was fighting Rebecca and her pack over the reporters. Carmella was not happy that Joshua was not done.

"Joshua, kill them already. We have more coming," She screamed.

Joshua shook his head and said to himself. "She is never happy, you know."

With that, Joshua looked back at Rebecca and the two members of her pack who were still alive. Rebecca howled at Joshua, signaling her pack mates to attack Joshua. All three of them ran at Joshua at the same time. Joshua just smiled and charged them.

Rebecca and Joshua's fight was being broadcast all over the world and the reporter was screaming his head off with a mix of shock and excitement seeing all this go down.

Just as Joshua and Rebecca and her pack hit each other, John and Edward and the pack came around the corner with the Calvary right behind them. The Bugler was sounding the charge as Morgan motioned Oscar and David towards the flagpole and where the captives were crucified.

Oscar and David, along with half the Calvary, went off to the right as Morgan charged towards city hall. Morgan and his men slammed right into Carmella's men coming off their horses as they hit the wall of men. Weapons are firing from both sides. It was bloody hand to hand combat. Morgan kept firing his FN_FAL rifle, ripping down ghoul and vampire alike as the royal guard behind him was fighting with sabers and Bullpup rifles. But Carmella's men were no pushovers as they fought back hard.

Oscar and David, with the Royal Guard, were in heavy combat. But Oscar and David knew what had to be done, and they fought with everything they had. More of the werewolves arrived and turned the tied to the fight as Carmella's men got pushed back. Oscar finally made it to the flagpole, took the Queens Battle standard, and raised it to the top of the mast.

The Reporter and Camera crew were able to keep sending a signal to the outside world, and with it, the Prime Minister, and his staff, along with his military advisors, saw the Queens Standard flying. The Prime Minister spit out his coffee when he saw it raised.

"What the hell is the Queen is there? And if so, where? And what about the coppers? Are they fixed yet?" The Prime Minister yelled.

David and his men finally made it to the captives. The guardsmen set up a defensive encircle while David saw to getting the Count, Baron, Mina, and Lily down. David helped the Count up and looked at him.

"I think this is yours. And when this is over, you and I are going to have a very long talk." David said to the Count as he handed the Count his sword.

The Count nodded to David. "I would like that, but it will have to wait. He said as he saw the police all come out of the Cathedral and attack Carmella's men.

Finally, the Baron, Mina, and Lily were free. The Baron was given his war hammer, and he did not hold back as Mina and Lily attacked

Carmella's men. Mina was not holding back. She showed why she was the Count's wife and how powerful she was as she bit and ripped Carmella's men apart.

"Carmella, where are you!" Mina screamed.

But then everyone heard a massive roar from above in the darkness of night. Carmella and Greggor looked up, as did everyone else. It looked as if the sky was on fire. Something was coming, and everyone was looking up. The cameraman tried to focus on the sky. It was nothing but fire coming in. Carmella pulled her sword as she pushed Greggor to get ready. Both were standing in front of the courthouse doors, looking up.

The cameraman could not believe what he was seeing, nor could the reporter who started to talk. "I don't believe what I am seeing; yes... we have vampires and what looks to be werewolves fighting. But now it seems, oh my God, it's. I can believe I am saying this or seeing it. But it's a Dragon. "The reporter said, stunned.

"What the hell!" The Prime Minister yelled at the Television screen.

Everyone looked shocked, seeing a Dragon flying in breathing fire. The Prime Minister looked at everyone. "Well, what else does this country have hiding in it?" He asked.

Everyone looked at each other, not sure how they did not know about a Dragon living in the country. More soldiers came over to see this Dragon, and they were all shocked at what they saw. The Dragon was massive. Its wingspan had to be a good two hundred feet across.

"You think the Dragon and Count were the reasons why the Germans never invaded during World War two?" A soldier asked.

Everyone looked at each other for a moment. For it could have been now that they thought about it. They knew the Count had made it known to the Germans, but if that Dragon was around, the Count knew it and kept it quiet. It would fit as a strong deterrent against any invasion. Even today, it would still scare anyone from invading the country. Just then, the camera caught two people on the Dragon.

"Oh, you got to be kidding. It can't be the Queen and the Prince, can it." The Prime Minister said.

Everyone kept watching as Carmella and Greggor also looked up to see them. Carmella looked over and saw her sister Mina coming up the stairs with Lily and then looked back up at the Dragon. Carmella was actually excited for the first time in a long time. She could smell blood and now could finally get more on her hands.

"Come on," Carmella said, smiling at the Dragon.

At that moment, the Dragon breached his wings, opened wide, and pulled him up to an almost stop. That was the moment Mary had waited for as she and Albert came of Night Star in full armor. They hit Carmella and Greggor hard, and all four went through the doors into the City Hall Rotunda area.

Joshua was deep in a fight with Rebecca and her two pack mates while the Dragon made its presence known. The Dragon kept hovering above the battleground, looking for opportunities to attack, but everyone was in hand to hand combat, and he knew that the Queen would be mad if he attacked her guards.

David was with Oscar at the flagpole fighting the vampires when the police force arrived. Chief Ludwig was leading them as they all met up together. David looked to the Chief and nodded.

"Good to see you again, Chief Ludwig," David said.

"Good to see you again as well, Sheriff. But I wish it would have been under better circumstances." The Chief replied.

Just then, a wave of Carmella's men attacked their position. Oscar laid down some cover fire as more officers attacked the vampires. The fighting was intense and hand to hand in some places. The police force was holding its own but was slowly losing footing.

The Count saw what was going on and whistled to the Baron, Mina, and Lily. Mary would have to fight on her own for a while. The four of them returned to the area near the flagpole and hit Carmella's men from behind.

Mina had the unique ability to break her body up into hundreds of bats and incased several vampires, killing them from her bites. When her body reformed, her long black hair shimmered in the moonlight. As her eyes glowed red, she kept going after more and more of her sister's men. Her anger was on full display as she really wanted to finally get a hold of her sister once and for all. But she was still her husband's wife, and he was not only her husband but also her sire. Her sister would have to wait.

Lily was with her husband, the Baron, supporting him as he ran headlong into a good twenty of Carmella's men. His massive war hammer pounded them to dust one after the other. The Baron did not realize that the hammer was a blessed gift but only a gift from Tarja. Each hammer hit caused one of Carmella's Vampires to burst into dust.

The Baron looked at his wife. "I love this hammer!" He yelled.

Lily smiled at her husband. "Have not seen you having this much fun in ages," She said.

Carmella's soldiers stopped and looked at Lily as she spoke and then realized they were doing nothing to the Baron. Fear ran throughout their minds as to what was going on. They were Vampires, lesser ones but still Vampires, so how could this creature plow right through them.

John and Edward were now in the fight with the pack. Their claws and teeth were shredding vampires left and right. But then Edward heard a click noise and looked down.

"Run!" was all Edward could say as the explosive went off, knocking him and the pack back against a building. Chief Ludwig saw the explosion and Carmella's men starting to break and run. He looked over at his second in command and nodded.

"Do it!" Chief Ludwig yelled

With that order, explosions went off all around the city. The underground tunnels that keep the river cavern under the city from collapsing exploded, bringing the whole area down into the caverns as the water rushed over everything in the tunnels, now making the city's heart an island. David and Oscar looked at the Chief. The Chief fired at two vampires close to them.

"We can't let any of these vampires escape," The Chief said.

Oscar looked to David and just nodded in understanding as they all went back to fighting.

Edward and Jon got up and shook the dust off themselves as they looked around. Just then, they saw Rebecca in a fight with a short man. The man (Joshua) was dogging Rebecca's attacks and laughing at her.

"Oh, come on, your support to be the badass alpha female around here. "Joshua said, mocking Rebecca.

Joshua knew all about Rebecca, the oldest daughter of the king of werewolves. He knew her fighting style and that she focused more on right claw attacks. Rebecca was playing right into the hands of her adversary. Due to Joshua's size, he was getting inside of Rebecca's claw strikes and hitting her with pricks and small slashes all on her right side. Rebecca was getting frustrated with this little man. How was he so fast, and why could she not hit him. She knew she had to do something, or she would lose. Not just that, but the reporters and her packmates would all die if she lost.

As all the explosions went off, Joshua's fighting changed as he had to hurry and get to Carmella to aid her. Joshua's smile faded, and he looked at Rebecca.

"Sorry, love, no more playtime, now time to die," Joshua said.

Rebecca charged Joshua. It was all she had thought that might work, but as she tried to claw Joshua. Joshua pivoted to his right as he knew Rebecca would lead with her right claw and let his blade slice her deep across her stomach's right side.

Rebecca winced in pain as she dropped to her knees, holding her side. She could feel blood on her claw. The pain and damage were enough to have Rebecca return to human form. Joshua starts walking towards her. The reporter and camera crew were close and kept filming.

"Got to say you were fun, but all things come to an end, So all I can say is time to die," Joshua said, laughing.

Joshua stood over Rebecca, holding up the blade he had sliced her all over. Rebecca looked up at him with anger, blood coming from her mouth. Joshua just smiled. But as he was bringing down the blade to kill Rebecca, he felt something hit his side.

Joshua looked down and saw a blade in his side and stumbled back in shock. As he stumbled back, the camera crew caught who through it. It was Jay Lester Morgan, the Queen's First Knight. He had made it just in time. Joshua pulled the blade out and dropped to the ground looking at Morgan.

"Who the hell are you," Joshua said for once, not knowing who Morgan was.

Morgan kept walking as he pulled his Katana, and Wakizashi looked right at Joshua. "I am Jay Lester Morgan, The Queen Mary Jade VonStines First Knight, and I will end your reign of terror tonight," Morgan said, his face showing no emotions.

The camera crew zoomed in on Morgan and the Shield on his left shoulder, the crest of the Queen. The Prime Minister looked at everyone.

"When did the Queen get a First Knight?" The Prime Minister asked.

No one could answer since this was the first time, they had seen Morgan. The reporter, who had not talked for a while, finally broke his silence.

"It seems the Queen's army is here, and now the one calling himself the Queens First Knight has come to face this monster who whipped out all these werewolves. I am sorry for not speaking up, but so much is going on that it's just best to let the camera tell the story. All we know is his name is Jay Lester Morgan, and he is standing alone against this monster who is dead set on killing us all." The reporter said with excitement.

Oscar finally saw Morgan up on the steps and took off to aid him. David and Chief Ludwig laid down cover fire for Oscar as he ran to help Morgan.

# 20

# Mary vs Carmella

Mary, Albert, Carmella, and Greggor came crashing through the doors of City Hall. They all four rolled into the center of the middle of the dome and stood up. Mary started to walk around with Albert was in his full Horus Paladin armor, Mary was in her fully activated black cat-like armor.

Carmella pulled off her skirt and held her sword out as Greggor stood up with his sword drawn. For Carmella, this was the first time seeing Mary and Albert in their armor. It caught her off guard, and it took her a moment to figure out what was happening.

"Well, well, if it isn't Queen Mary in all her Glory. I must say I do like your armor. Did your grandmothers give it to you?" Carmella said.

Mary's helmet folded back for a moment. Mary's eyes meet Carmella's. "Actually, they did." She replied.

Carmella was shocked.

Mary knew what Carmella was doing and started to play the same game. "What's wrong, Carmella, or should I call you his Bride," Mary said.

"What did you say? "Carmella said as she looked at Mary.

"What you did not think I knew about the other Master Vampire. The one you belong to." Mary said again, trying to get into Carmella's head.

Carmella's eyes locked on Mary as she was getting angry now. Mary smiled, seeing Carmella's expression. Mary pointed her finger at Carmella and tilted her head.

"Oh yes, I know all about him. He is the most famous Vampire after all. Tell me, were you around when Bram visited and wrote his book. Oh, come on, you can tell me, what you been with him now five hundred years. He must really love you. And you just whipped out all his army. For what just to kill the Count." Mary told Carmella.

Carmella's eyes glowed red as she was getting even angrier. "You know nothing of what happened. Your Count made a promise to protect my family. But all he did was protect my sister after he married her. The Turks raped me for days. Where was the Count? He was nowhere, no army, no nothing. I was almost dead when Tempest found me and gave me my chance for revenge. "Carmella yelled.

"Oh, stop lying, Carmella. I found the letters my ancestor sent to your father informing him to pull everyone to the royal castle. I also know when all that you talk of went down. My ancestor was dead, and the Count was lying on the ground dying. So, who was actually at fault for what happened to you? Oh, that's right, your own father failed you. It was his vanity that doomed you, not my family." Mary said.

Greggor kept listening to Carmella and Mary talk, but his eyes were on Albert. He had no information on him nor that armor. The more he watches Albert, the more he tries to read him with no luck. Greggor didn't like this at all. All this made no sense and puts him and his mother at a significant disadvantage.

But Carmella had enough of the talking and lashed out at Mary. Carmella's attack on Mary was a signal to Greggor to go after Albert. But Albert was waiting for the attack and easily parried Greggor with his swords. Greggor could not believe what had happened. No one had ever been his equal in speed. Albert stood there, his blades to his side, and looked at Greggor, not saying a word.

Carmella clashed with Mary. Carmella, full of anger, tried to slash Mary with her sword, but Mary's armor kept brushing it off. Mary then would pop her claws and just miss clawing Carmella. Carmella pulled back to rethink what had just happened.

"What the, when did you get claws, you're not a werewolf, "Carmella screamed.

Mary stood there holding up one of her hands, her black claw in view. Mary looked at Carmella. "I am my Grandfathers granddaughter after all," Mary said.

Carmella played it off and went back on the attack. This time ready for the claws, and this time she kept her anger in check. Mary was quickly on her heels as Carmella was quite good with a sword, and Mary only had her training with her Grandmothers. Carmella swept in with her sword but turned just at the last moment and hit Mary with a closed fist to the side of Mary's head.

Though the punch hit Mary in the head, the helmet took most of the blow. Still, she sent Mary flying almost into Albert. Mary landed on her feet in a four point stance just beside Albert. Albert was also backed up by Greggor. Clearly, they were a little overmatched, but they had no choice and had to really work as a team.

Mary looked back at Albert, "We have to take this to the temple. So, you have to keep him busy. Don't worry about Carmella throwing me around. It will be okay." Mary whispered to Albert.

Albert just nodded in agreement as Greggor, and Carmella moved in. But this time, Mary moved more cat-like and went right at Carmella. Albert went right at Greggor, keeping both swords he had in a low X formation so one would slice up and to the right as the other went to the left and low.

Greggor was surprised as he tried to attack and did not expect a charge. His sword went and blocked the upward swing but the lower one sliced into his thigh, cutting him but not deep enough to really do damage. Greggor turned, screaming as he pulled back with a sword up. His hand grabbed his leg and looked down.

Carmella could not look over at her son as she had to deal with Mary, who was right up at her. She was surprised how fast Mary had come in at her. Mary actually was able to slice Carmella just before

Carmella knocked her away into a corner of the room. Carmella ran over to Greggor to see what was wrong.

Greggor was still bleeding, and it did not heal like the wounds he got in battle all the time. This was the first wound he could not instantly heal from. Carmella looked and was shocked and looked over at Albert and saw the blood on one of his blades. Carmella thought for a moment and then over at Mary, who was getting up. She saw Mary's claw scratch the wall in the corner as she was standing.

Carmella started to put it together. "So that's it. I forgot you're a Demi-god for a moment, and my guess is your hubbies swords were made by the same ones who made your armors." Carmella said, looking at Mary and Albert.

Greggor looked over at Mary and Albert. "So holy weapons and armor that really are holy. Just great. "Greggor said.

Mary decided not to wait anymore and charged again with Albert right behind her. Greggor rolled to the left side and just was able to dodge Albert's attacks. Greggor pulled his sword and swept Albert's legs out from under him. But Albert rolled quickly to his left and back, rolling up on his feet with swords still in a defensive pose.

Mary was on Carmella again, but Carmella let Mary get close and then caught her and threw Mary over herself as Carmella rolled backward. "Not this time, girl!" Carmella yelled.

Mary hit the ground, rolling forward into another corner. Her claw racked the corner wall as she turned and went after Carmella again. Carmella noticed something Mary was not talking, and her breathing was not fast. Something did not make sense, and Carmella could not figure it out. But at the moment, she had to fight and worry about it later.

Carmella once again caught Mary and tossed her again into another corner of the room. Greggor slowed some as he kept up a good fight with Albert though he was having some issues with one sword versus two swords. He had to do something about that.

Albert kept making the same motions, and Greggor finally figured out his fighting style. And when Albert did the double slash, Greggor stepped forward between the blades and elbowed Albert in the face, which made Albert drop one of his swords. Greggor stopped as Albert stumbled back a few steps. Greggor bent down to pick up Albert's sword, but it would not come off the ground. No matter how Greggor tried, the sword would not move.

"You got to be kidding. It's bound to you as well. Gesh, what the hell are you two. You're sure, not humans, that's for sure." Greggor snarled.

Albert shook his head and went at Greggor, but Greggor kept Albert from his blade on the ground. Their swords swished and clashed back and forth as Albert kept Greggor out of Mary's way.

Mary clawed another corner now, she only had one more, and she hoped that Carmella had not figured out what she was doing. Carmella was coming after Mary now. Even though Mary had taken no slashes or cuts, her body was bruised due to all the throws she had taken. But she still had to get to the last corner of the room. Mary just barely dodged Carmella's charge and rolled to the side. Now, she had an open line to the far corner and took off for it.

Carmella turned and watched Mary run to the corner and looked around the room. "What are you...." She said, and then it hit her.

"Stop her, Greggor!" Carmella yelled.

Greggor turned, seeing Mary running to the corner, and started to run after her but forgot about Albert, who came up behind and sliced the back of his wounded leg. Greggor felt it burn bad, and he fell forward just short of catching Mary. Greggor rolled to get up to keep Albert away from him even though he missed Mary.

"No!!!!" Carmella screamed as she ran after Mary.

Mary made it to the corner and looked at everyone as her claw raked the corner. "Let's take this someplace else, shall we, "Mary said.

With that, everything went bright inside city hall, and everyone vanished.

# 21

# The First Knights
# Moment of Glory

Lawton, Oklahoma, The sun was shining over the city near the regional airport sits an apartment complex. In one of the units, two children are watching television. On the television was the live feed from Boldovia. As the two children watched, a girl around twelve years old and her younger brother around age ten, they see Jay Lester Morgan walking up towards the small man who had taken out all the werewolves.

Both children gasp, and the young girl got up and runs to the kitchen screaming. "Grandma, Grandma umpa Jay is on TV!"

As the young girl comes into the kitchen screaming, a little lady with long white hair in a ponytail looks at her in a soft voice. "What? What did you say, Kitty?" She asked

Kitty ran up to her Grandmother, pulling on her arm. "Umpa Jay is on TV. Come quick."

The elderly lady nodded "Okay, Kitty, Okay, I am coming," She said to get the girl to calm down.

The elderly lady walked into the room and saw Jay on the TV and stood there for a moment. She looked around. "Dear, Dear! get in here quick Jay is on TV." The elderly lady screamed.

An elderly man walking with a cane came from a back bedroom, looking at his wife. "What, What did you say, Dawn?" He said.

The elderly lady pointed at the TV. "It's Jay. He's on TV," she said.

The elderly man walked over, sat down in his recliner chair, and looked at the large TV.

"Okay, what's going ..." The elderly said but stopped in mid-sentence.

The man sat there, not saying a word, watching intensely what was on the TV. The Reporter started to talk again.

"Again, everyone, we are broadcasting live in the city of Teveahna, in the country of Boldovia. What you are seeing is real. This is live and uncut. I have never seen anything like this as it seems Vampires and Werewolves are real, and not just that but so are Dragons." The Reporter Reported as the camera pans up to show the massive Dragon in the air.

The elderly man looked closely at the TV. "It's real. It's really real. Dad was telling the truth all this time." He said as he saw the Dragon on the TV.

"What dear, what did you say?" The elderly lady asked.

"The Dragon is the one dad saw during the war. That has to be it. It has to. Dad really saw a Dragon back then." The Elderly man said but stopped as he saw Morgan walking towards the smaller man on the screen.

"Jay, what are you doing there," The elderly man said.

As Jay was getting closer, everyone heard Morgan say. "I am Jay Lester Morgan, Queen Mary Jade VonStines First Knight, and I will kill you. Your murderous ways end tonight, little man."

The elderly man looked at his wife. "When did Jay become a knight? What is going on?" he asked.

The elderly woman looked at him. "I don't know, dear, Jay has not come home in years."

The elderly man went back to watching the TV and paid close to its action. Morgan and Joshua charged each other. To Joshua's surprise, Morgan was just as fast and, in fact, was better than him at fighting. Morgan landed three hits on Joshua right off the bat. His blades hit home all three times.

Joshua winched from the cuts and turned and looked at Morgan. "Oh, you're good, very good, but you can't kill me." He said to Morgan as his body healed the cuts.

"You want a surprise? I will tell you a surprise." Joshua said but was interrupted by Morgan.

"You're a Gargoyle. I know you're an ancient monster and not a vampire. You can still die, and I know exactly how to kill you." Morgan said.

Joshua was shocked by what Morgan had just said. "Oh, your fun, yes, your correct I am a Gargoyle but not an ordinary one, fool. I am blood bound to Carmella. So, you should know I am truly immortal. But you. You're out of place, First Knight, you're not European; you're something else. What are you? Hmmm. "

Morgan keeps moving forward towards Joshua, and the camera crew was focused on this fight and picking up every word. Morgan moved in again, but he did something out of place as they fought this time. Morgan hit Joshua in the face with the butt of his sword, not the blade.

"I am the First Knight, but I am also a Comanche Warrior and the son of Chief Wahoo Rainstorm," Morgan said.

The elderly man pounded his staff on the floor. "Take him down, Jay," He said. His voice was full of pride.

Everyone looked at the elderly man. He had not spoken like that in years. Wahoo, keep focused on that fight saying over and over. "Come on. Son, keep at it."

Joshua was at a loss. He did not even know what the word Comanche was or who those warriors were. But it did not matter. He was having fun with this fight. For once, someone who could really fight him, and it gave him a rush. A rush he had not felt in years.

"Come on, then let's fight, "Joshua yelled.

Morgan gave Joshua what he wanted. Morgan moved in and again hit Joshua with several slices from his swords. Joshua came back and finally hit Morgan, sending him flying towards the camera crew and Rebecca's pack. Morgan rolled as he hit the ground and came up in a three-point stance.

Morgan went right back after Joshua. He came in again low and fast, and Joshua tried to block it, but Morgan's blade hit true, and this time the cut did not heal for some reason. Joshua looked down and then to Morgan and back down at the wound.

"Hmmm, well, that's new," Joshua said.

Morgan looked at the cut and looked around, and then smiled as he saw the little black cat with white paws show up. Joshua looked over to what Morgan was smiling at. "Oh, you got to be kidding me," Joshua said.

The black cat with white paws just looked at both men and walked over by Rebecca and stretched and then laid down and looked at the fighters.

Joshua looked down and started to laugh. "You know this night has really sucked." He said.

"Your right," Morgan said as his Wakizashi hit Joshua right in the middle of his face.

Joshua stepped back with the blade in his head. His head tilted to the side as his hand came up, pulled the sword out, and dropped it on the ground. Joshua waved a finger at Morgan as his head regenerated the wound. "Nice try, but no, I can't be killed that easily. You thought you could be sneaky, so now the gloves come off, my dear boy. I am older than even that flying monster up in the air and all around here. I am one of the five original children of Lilith, the first Demon." Joshua boasted.

"Nothing is ever simple, is it," Morgan said.

Joshua cracked his neck, and then his skin turned dark red as horns grew out of his head. His whole body grew bigger and larger till he was eight feet tall. Joshua's face grew more lizard-like with a long snout and jagged teeth. His eyes went back in his head as they changed to a yellow color. His back sprouted wings large red demon wings. His arms grew massive in size, with his hands now more like claws. Joshua really was a Demon right out of the pits of hell.

Back in Lawton, Chief Wahoo kept watching and again slammed his cane on the ground. "Stand up, my son, stand and be counted.

Fight for all of us. Never back down. You are Comanche now fight like one." He said with pride in his voice.

Everyone in the room was shocked. They had not heard Wahoo speak like this in a long time. Just then, more of the family came in with groceries. "Mom, Dad, come quick Umpa Jay is on TV in a fight. The young girl ran over." She yelled.

The couple came in and saw everyone around the TV. As they looked on, they saw Joshua transform into the Demon Gargoyle he was and Jay standing with a sword in front of him. "What the hell is going on. "The mother said.

Chief Wahoo looked to his Daughter. "Jay is fighting to save people. He is showing he is a warrior." Chief Wahoo said with pride to her.

Joshua roared at Morgan. Morgan charged at the Demon and went right at him. Morgan was still fast and able to dodge Joshua's attacks. He sliced him repeatedly, trying to find the right spot that would weaken Joshua.

Oscar looked over and saw Morgan in trouble and took off over to help his friend. Chief Ludwig and Sherriff Phillips gave him cover fire as the rest of the VonStine family worked up the courthouse steps. But more and more of Carmella's men were intercepting them and keeping them at bay so that the fights could continue, for no one knew what was going on inside the courthouse after that blinding light.

As Oscar got closer, he opened up with his Bullpup assault rifle, hitting Joshua with several rounds. As Joshua arched his back from being hit by bullets, Morgan came up under Joshua and sliced his stomach, trying to gut him. But Joshua was an actual demon, and the slice did nothing to him. As he looked down at Morgan, he brought both of his massive claws clasped together in an ax hit, knocking Morgan to the ground. As Morgan slowly got up, Joshua kicked Morgan in the Stomach area.

You could hear Morgan's ribs break from the blow as he went flying back towards the camera crew and where Rebecca and her pack were lying badly wounded. The camera crew kept moving and focusing on the fight. As Morgan got up, spitting blood, he looked at Joshua. His hand gripped his Katana, and he attacked Joshua again.

Oscar again laid down suppression fire on Joshua, hitting him several times. However, Joshua was ready and cupped his wings around him to block the shots.

Joshua was brilliant and could only be fooled once. He knew Morgan was coming as his partner had laid down fire on him. But just as Morgan got to Joshua. Joshua spun around, and his claw came up under Morgan and went into Morgan's midsection.

Morgan Gasped, feeling the hit, and spit up blood. Joshua smiled as his snake-like tongue licked at Morgan's blood. "You are the best fighter I have ever faced, Comanche. But all good things must come to an end. Joshua said.

But just then, Oscar jumped on Joshua's back and stabbed him. Joshua bucked back, throwing Morgan down to the ground near the camera crew.

Chief Wahoo screamed at the TV, "GET UP, JAY! GET UP!" and slammed his cane to the ground.

Everyone in the room was shocked by how Chief Wahoo was acting. Chief Wahoo was out of his chair and right at the TV.

"Come on, son. You can do this. Come on, get up. Son, get up." Chief Wahoo said emotionally.

Just then, Morgan got up, blood coming from his mouth, breathing had become hard for him as he looked at Joshua, thinking. Oscar was all over Joshua as he kept firing his assault rifle and dodging his attacks. But finally, Joshua caught Oscar and pulled him up to where they were face to face.

Joshua smirked at Oscar. "You're a pest. You know that." Joshua told Oscar.

Oscar laughed at Joshua and looked over at Morgan and winked. Oscar then looked at Joshua face to face. "Ya, I may be a pest. But your dead." Oscar said to Joshua.

Morgan saw the wink and yelled, "NO!"

But it was too late as Oscar raised his right hand and pushed a button on it. "Sorry, Boss see you in the next life," Oscar said.

Joshua's eyes went big as he saw Oscar push the button. The button set off a set of C-4 explosives Oscar had around his body. The explosion knocked everyone back and many off the courthouse steps.

Morgan was severely hurt, bleeding down his mid area and legs, broken ribs, and blood from his mouth stood up. He was trying to breathe, but it was difficult to do so. The camera crew was up with the Reporter and back to filming.

"He did it. They won... the First...." The Reporter stopped talking in mid-sentence to everyone's horror. Joshua was up to his knees. Joshua was missing his left arm. His right arm was hanging down, and half his face was gone. Both his wings were missing as well. But his body was starting to regenerate.

Morgan knew his time was short and looked up seeing Night Star. Morgan nodded to Night Star to follow his actions. Night Star noticed everyone was away from Joshua and watched Morgan closely.

Morgan walked towards Joshua, his hands together, holding something. Morgan looked face to face with Joshua and hauled back and punched Joshua in the face repeatedly. Morgan sent his fist one more time to hit Joshua, but Joshua had regenerated just enough to catch Morgan's fist and part of his arm in his mouth.

Joshua bit down hard and ripped Morgan's arm off. He then hit Morgan with an uppercut punch sending him back into Rebecca and her pack, who were almost healed enough to get up.

Morgan laid there coughing up blood but slowly stood up. Morgan was a mess how he was standing but no one knew how. Morgan looked at Joshua and coughed up more blood.

Joshua swallowed Morgan's arm and laughed. "Good try but way too short. I win. I always... "Joshua stopped mid-sentence seeing Morgan raise his left hand, and on his ring, finger was the pin, a little ringlike tab.

"No. I win," Morgan said.

Joshua looked down. "Oh Hell" is all he said before the grenade went off, blowing up his midsection.

Morgan looked up at Night Star. "Do it now, big guy," Morgan yelled as he fell back into Rebecca's arms.

Morgan knew Joshua would regenerate and be right back up to fight in no time. But this time was different, and Night Star finally let loose. Dragon fire rained down on Joshua as it lit up the whole sky. Night Star did not stop. He kept the fire coming, and it was hot. The small amount of sand on the steps was turning into glass. It was so hot. Joshua's body tried to fight it and regenerate. Still, the flames keep coming, getting hotter and hotter, melting the granite stones. Everyone around was feeling the heat and backing up.

Everyone in Lawton that was watching had to cover their eyes. The light from the flames was so bright. No one could tell what was going on. But they all knew Jay had won, and Chief Wahoo was proud of his son at last.

Night Star landed and roared as he turned and looked out over the square. The Count and the rest rushed up to stairs fighting Carmella's men, but her men had lost the motivation to keep fighting and soon were routed.

# 22

# The Final Judgement

Carmella looked around as she found herself and her son at the main hall of Karnack and the great temple itself. Sitting at the end of the main hall was Anubis and to each side was Bastet and Sek-Met with Horus off to the side standing. Carmella screamed loudly "No No you are forbidden from getting involved."

But Anubis raided his hand to silence Carmella.

"We are not here to Judge you Carmella Duchess of Valmor, we are here to just observe and take note is all. The one who you face now is your judge and will judge you accordingly if you should lose." Anubis proclaimed.

Carmella was taken back as she turned and looked at Mary and to her surprise, Mary's armor changed the helmet became more cat-like and her boots changed to be like they were when she spared with the Goddesses. Carmella still had her sword and had already seen Mary with her claws from the start of the fight. But now Carmella was facing Mary as she had really become.

Mary quickly moved to the right then to the left. She had become ten times as fast as she was in the courthouse and Carmella could barely keep up with her eyes. But Carmella had tricks of her own and so she did not stay on defense but went to office and caught Mary by surprise as her sword hit home but it did not hurt Mary. In fact, Mary's armor was more than a match for Carmella's sword.

While Mary and Carmella was going at it. Greggor and Albert were also going at it. As Greggor's broadsword and Alberts two swords clashed. Even though Greggor was a master swordsman he was having issues with Albert all this made not since to him. How did Albert get this good and where did he get this armor. Greggor knew Albert was in the Boldovian army, but they did not teach swordsmanship at all.

Greggor had to do something and so he keep pushing with more thrusts to push Albert towards the main pillared hall so to use the pillars as an advantage and split up Albert from Mary. For Albert had keep in a way stepping in somehow and taking sword strikes from Carmella as well.

Mary and Albert both figured out what Greggor was trying to do so switched their own actions in which out of nowhere Mary rolled under Albert and caught Greggor off guard as her claws racked the insides of both of Greggor's thighs. Greggor screamed as he felt the claws cut both the insides of his thighs. He would stager back out of the fight for the moment lucky that Mary did not cut the arteries in his thighs.

Now Mary and Albert behind her focused-on Carmella and Carmella could tell they were coming. But now Carmella did something out of the counts play book and as Mary came at her Carmella's body broke into hundreds of bats and she attacked Albert.

Albert and Mary were both caught off guard by this attack and both of them panicked for a moment. But that was all Carmella needed to reform and knock Albert into one of the pillars, making it collapse on top of him. Albert was now trapped for now under a collapsed pillar, and Greggor was out of the fight with both inner thighs sliced open and needing time to heal. So, it was just Carmella and Mary facing each other.

Mary slowly walked around Carmella just out of swords reach. "Nice trick but it will only work once" Mary said. Carmella smiled "Oh I know dear and have to say you and your husband are full of surprises as well. Nice armor and that Dragon of yours. How did you keep that big thing hidden all these years. I am guessing it belonged to the great prince." Carmella said.

Mary keep looking for a moment to attack but for now she could not do anything but keep talking. "Oh, you mean Night Star, Yes, he did belong to my ancestor, and he stayed in the treasure room which only I know where it is. "Mary replied.

Carmella was shocked "Wait what treasure room" She replied. Which was all Mary needed for Carmella let her guard down just for a moment and Mary struck. Carmella came out of her daze just in time she thought to dodge Mary's claws. And tried to attack Mary as she went by but missed. Mary looked over her shoulder at Carmella and Carmella laughed at her "Nice try but your several hundred years too young to catch me off guard." Carmella said. But to Carmella' surprise Mary held up her left hand as she turned and to face her. Carmella was shocked. Mary's claw was stained red with blood. Carmella looked down and saw her blouse ripped open and her stomach bleeding.

Camella was shocked to the fact she could not heal instantly from the strike like she could with any other attack. Then it hit her Mary was a demigod and so partly divine, so her claws were like holy weapons. Carmella had taken Mary for just a young child who could not fight but could boast now she knew different.

As Mary looked at Carmella. Carmella heard a loud yell behind her and turned to see Albert land a blow on Greggor the blow was to Greggor's left arm and it almost took it off. Greggor stepped back as he still had his sword in his right hand. Greggor as a Vampire was easily strong enough to use the sword with just his right hand. But Greggor knew he was running out of time if he took another hit like that he would be done for. But how did Albert get so strong and how even with his military training how was it he could use the swords like he was doing.

Horus was watching Albert closely to see how well he had learned from his teachings and was very surprised how well he had picked everything up.

Bastet and Sek-Met were fidgeting while they watched Carmella and Mary fight, but Anubis keep reminding them they could not get involved.

As the Gods watched on it was clear that Albert was getting the upper hand on Greggor and that Greggor missing an arm was in deep trouble. Carmella ever so often could see what was going on but could not do anything for she herself was back on her heels against Mary. This was not what Carmella had planned and not just that Mary was not what Carmella had expected.

Mary was moving in and out on the tips of her feet and she was fast her claws keep getting close to Carmella, but Carmella was able to perry or dodge but just by a split second. Mary looked at Carmella "What's the matter Aunt Carmella you seemed worried and flustered and poor Greggor already lost an arm I see. But he is lasting longer than Demitriof did. "Mary said trying to bate Carmella.

Carmella stopped and looked at Mary "What did you say?" Carmella yelled at Mary. Mary just pointed behind Carmella. Carmella turned to see just now arriving was none other than Hades and Persephone and with theme was Demitriof, but it was his soul not his body.

Carmella was in raged and lashed out at Mary and Mary was ready as Mary keep playing now with Carmella who had totally lost her focus seeing her dead son's soul standing with the God Hades she was in a mind of anger and rage.

As Mary and Carmella keep fighting Greggor had let his guard down a second time and this time it was fatal as Carmella heard Greggor scream and turned just at the moment Albert's swords sliced Greggor in two right down the middle. Carmella screamed as she saw her son fall and die in front of her. This was now a nightmare to her and when she turned back to face Mary her breath was cut short.

Mary had moved in and as Carmella had turned back around Mary's claw had rammed into Carmella's body just under the ribs and had come up to wrap around Carmella' heart. Mary was right up to Carmella. Carmella was shocked as her breath was quick and shallow. Her eyes were wide as she looked into Mary's.

"If you remember Anubis said he would not judge you and he did speak the truth for even in this land you are still a citizen of Boldovia and for that only I can judge you dear Aunt Carmella." Mary said.

Carmella was in shock she had totally forgotten that she was after five hundred years still part of the kingdom. Carmella could not talk her body shacked as Mary held her heart in her hand.

Finally, Mary spoke "At this moment you and I see your whole life and what was real and what was a lie. We see what really happened back in the days before you became a Vampire and all the pain and suffering you suffered. With all the lies you believed and all those you destroyed in believing those lies. You see why the Prince and Count never saved you and how your own Father lied about things to start with." Mary said.

Carmella had tears in her eyes seeing everything she believed was a lie and everyone she thought were her enemy and hated her was in truth never that way she had spent all those years full of rage for no reason. Only the one who made her a vampire cared about her and he would give her everything in the end she did not see how much he loved her. But now that's over and see looked at Mary and saw Mary now more as her niece and how beautiful she was. "I am so.. sorry Mary but it's too late now please forgive me." Carmella whispered to Mary as tears rolled down her face.

Mary sighed "Carmella Diana Valmor I now pass judgement on you. I could forgive you if your actions were just on me and my family, but it is not. I sentence you to death but a peaceful and eternal rest with no pain, and both your son's will join you in your eternal slumber. "Mary said and with that Mary crushed Carmella's heart with her claws.

Carmella's eyes closed and as she collapsed Mary caught her and laid her down gently on the sand. Albert brought over Greggor's body and set it beside his mother. Albert went over and stayed beside Mary and gave her a hug. "Are you okay?" Albert asked Mary.

Mary looked to Albert and nodded "Yes I am fine." She replied.

Anubis finally brought his staff down and it rang over the temple as he stood up. Even Hades was surprised by the judgement but watched Anubis for this was his realm and Hades was just here to bring Demitriof for judgement. Anubis walked up to where Mary and Albert, along with the bodies of Greggor and Carmella were resting. Anubis looked at Mary, "You surprise me granddaughter tell me why you did your judgement like you did and not go for vengeance?" Anubis asked.

Mary looked up to Anubis and sighed "Yes, I wanted vengeance and I got it but on this I am still Queen of Boldovia, and I have to Judge by facts for facts don't care about my feelings and I must remember that when I make a ruling. That is what I did and why I did it. It was very hard to do it, but it was the right thing." Mary said to Anubis.

Anubis looked down at Mary "I approve you did right my granddaughter and your words are true." Anubis said as he walked over and held out his hand, and with that the souls of Greggor and Carmella stood up. Then Anubis looked over at Demitriof and Hades nodded to him to join his mother and brother, Anubis would then lead the three into the temple and after a few moments would return to the group.

Hades walked over to Mary and looked at her. "You are very interesting nothing like those of the past that were like you from Greece. It will be fun watching what you do next young one. We will keep a close eye on you that is for sure. "Hades said to Mary.

While Hades talked with Mary, Persephone walked over and looked to Bastet and Sek-Met, "please come visit some time it has been way to long since we all relaxed together." She said to Bastet and Sek-Met.

Both Bastet and Sek-Met nodded. "Oh yes it will be great it has been way to long since our last time we got together." Bastet said.

With that it was time to return and Mary and Albert and the bodies of Greggor and Carmella returned to the inside of the city hall rotunda, but it was not like they left it. The building was a total mess and in ruins.

Mary looked around and signed as she knew for the second time the city would have to be rebuilt but this time, she would bring her castle into the city and not on the mountain. Mary knew that her castle on the mountain was gone along with the manor house. Mary looked to Albert. "It's quiet I guess it's all over we best go outside." Mary said as her helmet vanished into her armor, Albert nodded and his helmet as well vanished. With that Albert and Mary walked to the doors leaving Carmella and Greggor's body lying on the ground. Albert looked to Mary and smiled.

"Whatever happens I will always be at your side." Albert said to Mary.

Mary smiled and gave her husband a kiss. "I will aways be with you." Mary replied.

# 23

# The World Learns the Truth

The city of Teveahna laid in ruins as the whole downtown area was totally destroyed. The great statue fountain in the center along with the train station was nothing but rubble with a massive dragon standing on it.

The news reporter and his team were in disbelief that they lived through the carnage and had reported it all live. In his voice the reporter was shaking but able to give a report as he looked around at everything.

"I have never seen anything like what has taken place tonight who would believe that monsters like these lived in this land. Your eyes do not play tricks on you what you see is all real from that massive dragon to the werewolves to the vampires and all the soldiers it's all real and this was a war that took place here.

We still do not know the condition of the queen or her husband. But we hope it's all over and everything is finally safe. "The reporter was fixing to continue but the courthouse doors opened and walking out in her armor with her helmet off was the Queen Mary Jade VonStine and beside her was her husband Prince Albert VonStine in his armor with his helmet off as well. Near the doors was the Count, the Baron, Lily, and Mina the four all sighed a sign of relief seeing them walk out.

The Count asked as he looked to Mary what happened. And Mary looked to the count and then to the people who were all standing looking at her. "Carmella has fallen and the war she started five hundred years ago is finally over. We must now look to our wounded and see to the civilians who are in need of help as well." Mary stated to all around.

David and Chief Ludwig came up to Mary and the rest. David looked tired as he looked around" Mary you alright?" he asked.

Mary smiled and nodded and gave David a hug very relieved he was alive and well. As Mary looked around at all who came up, she did not see Morgan her knight. "where is my Knight?" Mary asked.

Rebecca waved over to Mary to come to her. Mary and the rest walked over to Rebecca as the news team followed. The reporter really wanted to ask some questions but had to wait as they stopped near Rebecca. For laying in Rebecca's lap was Morgan's head resting his body was broken up really bad and he knew his time was short. Mary knelt down beside him and took his hand.

"Well looks like we won your majesty." Morgan said as he coughed up blood. Mary had tears in her eyes seeing Morgan like this and knew nothing could be done.

"You did your duty my Knight." Mary said trying to be strong for Morgan. Morgan coughed up more blood as he smiled. "Good now I can go on without any regrets." Morgan said as he laid in Rebecca's lap. The Count walked over and looked down at Morgan. The Count knew the secret was out and did not care anymore what the world thought. "First Knight of the Queen, I offer you a choice stay with us and be the Queens First Knight for all times or" Morgan cut the count off.

"No Count I am not that honorable of a man but thank you. I am tired and I wish to return home to my people and rest with my ancestors for that is my peoples way. "Morgan said as he saw a light that no one else saw and Morgan saw Sek-Met standing there and then he saw her move to the side, and he saw the great chiefs of his people call to him and with that Morgan's eyes closed for the last time and he was gone his spirit with the warriors of his people for he had keep his promise and saved the queen and her people.

Chief Wahoo started to cry seeing his son die. But then he stood up and started to sing in Comanche a song of the warrior for his son had died a true Comanche Warrior this day.

Mary leaned over and kissed Morgan's forehead and softly spoke "Rest well my Knight you will always be remembered for what you have done this night." Mary said as she stood up. Mary would look around the square as she stood on the steps of what was left of city hall.

Finally, the reporter was able to say something "Your Majesty if you will, I have a lot of questions for you over what has taken place tonight and all the world has watched all this go down. So, if you would give us some information." The reporter asked Mary.

Mary looked to the reporter and smiled. "Very well its best to set all the records strait now before people make things up and it gets out of hand." Mary said.

The reporter could not believe this and for a moment composed himself as best he could, and the camera operator would make sure to get everything live. The report finally was ready. "To all who are watching this is Jeremy Reinferaoda of the Boldovia national news with me is her Royal Majesty Queen Mary Jade VonStine and as you have seen tonight, we have seen a battle for the country like no other with what we all thought were imaginary creatures who turned out to be very real as you can see." The reporter stated pointing at the massive dragon who had landed and was laying in the middle of the square.

"Your Majesty it seems all of the royal family are monsters from Vampires to Werewolves but what of you, are you also one of these monsters to be feared." The reporter asked Mary.

Mary smiled. "No, I am not a monster like my family. You see my ancestor the great Prince Edward and his younger brother who is standing over there fought to save the country in which the great prince my ancestor died, and his brother was wounded badly. On that day the prince's brother the count became a Vampire and made an oath to always protect the VonStine family and the country. In which he did for all this time.

But it would take a heavy toll on my family as the count and his family would all become vampires except for my Aunt Lillian's son who at birth was attacked by a werewolf and he was made one for all time. Everyone you saw fight tonight yes, they are monsters, but they are the protectors of Boldovia and have been for over five hundred years. This is why the Nazi's were not able to invade this small country for all the monsters as you call them fought against true evil just as they did tonight. The world may shun this country, but they are my people and my family, and I will never give them up and I will always defend the citizens of Boldovia. "Mary said to the reporter.

At which point the whole square cheered for hearing what Mary had said even Night Star roared with happiness as well.

Mary and the rest would now go and see how bad the city was and make sure the wounded were getting the help they needed. But Mary's heart was broken seeing everything destroyed and her castle was now totally gone. As the sun arose in the east the destruction was now fully visible, and it was so bad that Mary would be in tears seeing all this. As she and Albert walked the city with her family David and Chief Ludwig would be with them.

For the near future Mary and all the royal family would live at the VonStine Keep at Mirror Lake. From the VonStine Keep Mary along with her advisors use the treasure she had along with almost half of her whole fortune to come up with and pay for the cities total rebuild and she would have a new Castle as well for the city would rise out of its ashes and be a city that her country could be proud of.

As things went on the United Nations had met for since every country knew all along about the monsters and keep them secret, they were in a corner on what to do. The United Nations came up with the idea of a Resolution that called for Boldovia to become the sanctuary of mystical creatures would be how they put it. Putting in place that Boldovia would be the country of monsters and no country would make war against them and let them live in peace. Furth more they would set up a committee for monster affairs where they would aid in helping monsters relocate to Boldovia if they chose to.

Around the world historians went back and looked at old records and tails of monsters and dragons to see if they had any truth to them. Now that things had come to light in how many fables were real and really happened back in history.

# 24

# Aftermath

It had been three weeks since the attack on Teveahna Boldovia. The pass to the old capital was reopened, and a new train line was being put in. A new train station was temporarily being put in, but the new station would be near the outskirts of town at the crossroads.

A Chinook helicopter approached the main airport in the capital. It slowly turned on final and landed near the Royal Dreamliner that was waiting on the tarmac. The Chinook rolled to a stop, and the ground crews came and went through all the procedures to secure it. The side door of the Chinook opened.

Albert and Mary exited the Chinook and walked over to the Dreamliner. As they were walking over to the Dreamliner, the back of the Chinook opened, and the Royal Guard in full dress uniforms exited the Helicopter carrying a flagged draped casket. The Royal Guard would take the casket over to the plane and wait for it to be loaded before walking over to the entry of the Dreamliner.

Albert would escort Mary into the plane as the Guards would follow behind. After all, we're on board the plane, the cabin door would be shut, and the walkway would pull away from the Dreamliner. A few minutes later, the Dreamliner would taxi to the runway and then depart, flying south and turning to the west.

Lawton, Oklahoma, was a sunny but sad day as many townspeople and the honor guard from Fort Sill Military Base had gathered at the Regional Airport. They were there to welcome one of their own.

Out of the East, the silhouette of the Black Dreamliner slowly came into view. The Honor Guard waited at attention. In front of the Honor Guard was the Base Commander and Mayor of the City of Lawton. Everyone watched the Dreamliner turn on final and approach the air-port for landing. The Dreamliner would touch down and go to the end of the runway. The Royal Crest shined off the Tail of the Dreamliner as it turned to move up the tarmac to where the reception was stationed.

The Dreamliner would pull up to park, and its engines would throttle down. The ground crew would then move up to secure the Dreamliner, which was now safe to approach.

The jet bridge was rolled into place against the plane. The side door of the Dreamliner was opened, and members of the ground crew went in to make sure all was okay. Moments later, the ground crew would return to the base of the jet bridge.

Moments later, the Royal Guard would exit the aircraft and walk down the jet bridge to the ground. Then in formation, the Royal Guard would march to the back where the cargo bay was and stand at attention.

Next would come Velmar, who would come down the jet bridge and walk over to meet the Mayor and Base Commander. Velmar was dressed in a three piece black suit with purple tie.

"Good Ha ven," Velmar would say to them.

"Good day sir, "I am Mayor Phillip Running Dear, and this is General Mitchel Kilpatrick, Commander of Fort Sill."

The General would Shake Velmar's hand. "A Pleasure, Sir"

"Thank you for meeting us today," Velmar said.

"Of course, after all, you are bringing home one of our own," The Mayor said.

Everyone looked at the plane and the top of the jet bridge as Albert came out. He was in a black suit with a purple tie on. He looked out and then turned to face the entryway of the plane. Finally, the Queen came out. Mary was in a black dress with her hair in a long black po-nytail. Albert escorted Mary down the jet bridge to the waiting crowd.

The Mayor and General both welcomed her and Albert. At which point, a cane could be heard coming closer to them. It was Chief Wahoo who was there to receive his son's body.

The Mayor walked Mary and Albert over to meet Morgan's father.

"Chief Wahoo Rainstorm, may I Introduce Queen Mary Jade VonStine, Queen of Boldovia, and her husband, Prince Albert Ludwig VonStine." The Mayor said.

Chief Wahoo was in a black suit with a red tie on his eyes, looked at Mary, and smiled.

"Thank you for restoring my son's honor and bringing him home." Chief Wahoo said.

"It is my honor. Your son saved my country. I am sorry he sacrificed himself for my sake." Mary said as she put her hand on the Chiefs.

The Chief just smiled at Mary as the cargo door opened. Everyone turned as the Casket was lowered to the Royal Guard. The Royal Guard held the Casket as the Captain of the Guard put the Royal flag over it. The Captain of the Guard turned, and all the Royal Guard proceeded to march with the Casket to the crowd and the hurst that was waiting.

As the Casket was placed on the rollers to go into the hurst, the royal flag was removed and folded, and a United States flag was laid over the Casket, for Morgan had served with honor in the Army when he was younger. The funeral would be the next day, but formalities had to be made.

Morgan would lay in state at the First Baptist Church in Lawton for the night, and the service would be that afternoon followed by the gave side. But tonight, the drums would play and tribal dancing. The dancing was a first for everyone from Boldovia. Even though Mary had been born in the United States, she had never seen any native dancing before.

As Mary and Albert sat watching the show. Chief Wahoo kept looking at her for something seemed off about her. But then, out of no-where, the black cat with white paws came out of the darkness, walked over, and lay down in Mary's lap.

The Chief tapped his brother, who was sitting beside him, and nodded over at where Mary was sitting. The Chief's brother looked over, seeing the cat lying in Mary's lap and noticing it was just watching the dancing. This was very unusual, but it hit him that cats for the Comanche are totem animals who are guardians of the spirit, and he felt at ease with the cat. He was a shaman and understood the cat was here for a reason. But why was it with the Queen who was not Comanche and not near one of the tribe? He would think about it but never understand.

The Morning was perfect for the day to come, Mary and Albert had a quiet evening after the dancing, and now today, Mary was keeping her promise to her First Knight.

Velmar knocked on the door before meeting with the royal couple and going over the day's events. Mary and Albert would have breakfast before meeting with their guards and members of the city police who were doing security for them. The Chief of Police was surprised to find out Mary had been born and raised in the United States, and she still had her southern accent when she spoke English.

The time was 2 pm as the motorcade moved from the hotel to the church. The First Baptist Church was a lovely building with a high white spire and reddish brown bricks. The front doors were white, with an awning held up by white pillars. In front of the entrance, the hurst was parked behind the limo for the family, and then the royal limo was behind that. And several SUVs behind that.

As everyone came into the Church, the main auditorium was a circle with a balcony that wrapped around to a stage where the Pastor was standing. Morgan's Casket was at the base of the steps of the stage.

Everyone would come in and be seated as the Pastor would step up on the stage. The Royal Guard would come in from one side in their uniforms as the Army Honor Guard would come in from the other side.

Then Mary and Albert, with Velmar behind them, would come in and sit just to the left side of where the family would be seated. Finally, Chief Wahoo and his wife, followed by his other Son and Daughter with her Husband and their four children would walk in and be escorted to be seated.

After they were seated with more of the family, the Pastor would call the service to order and say a prayer to start. The Pianist would play an opening song. Then the Pastor would again say a prayer before turning the service over to the Fort Sill Base Commander.

The General would read over the service record of Morgan and what he did during his service and all the honors and awards he had been presented for his service. After the General had finished, the Pastor would say another prayer.

Then Mary would stand and come up to the stage. She was in a long black dress. Her hair was in her usual ponytail. She let a small smile show as she looked over at the crowd and Morgan's family.

Mary took a breath and then spoke. "I am Queen Mary Jade VonStine, the Queen of Boldovia. Jay Lester Morgan served as my First Knight. This title is only given to the very best of my Royal Guard. The Title makes the one who holds it Commander of all the Royal Guard and personal protector of the Ruler of Boldovia.

"Jay Lester Morgan led the Royal Guard, the wolf division of the Army, and the dragon Night Star into battle to save the country of Boldovia. During that battle, Jay would distinguish himself and sacrifice himself to save many innocent people who would have indeed died. In the end, he would cecum to his wounds and pass away on the battlefield. I could not have asked for a greater First Knight than Jay Lester Morgan." Mary said as a tear finally ran down her cheek. She would then leave the stage and return to her seat. The Pastor would say another prayer, and the Pianist would play another song. Finally, the Pastor would go through a short sermon about God's grace. The Pianist would play Amazing Grace to end the service.

The Family of Morgan would come by the Casket first and then the citizens of Lawton, and finally Mary, Albert, and the Base Commander. The Honor Guard and the Royal Guard would escort the Casket out of the Church and then place it in the hurst.

Everyone would get in their respective vehicles and follow behind the hurt to the cemetery for the Graveside. Again, the Royal Guard and the Honor Guard would escort Morgan's Casket to his Graveside. There it would sit while the Pastor would say a few words. The US Flag and the VonStines Royal Flag would be presented to Chief Wahoo. Chief Wahoo would hold on to both Flags as Morgan's Casket was lowered into the ground, and then the Pastor would close the ceremony. For the rest of the day, Morgan's family would celebrate his life and that he went out like a true warrior.

As night fell, the cat with white paws would come and sit near the headstone of Morgan. A lady with golden hair in a black dress would come as the cat sat licking its paw from the shadows. She would walk up to where Morgan rested and set a single lily flower on the dirt. She would then pick up the cat in her arms and turn. Chief Wahoo's brother would make his presence known as she walked away.

"I figured the cat was a Totem, But who are you, and why was it with the Queen? Something doesn't make sense." He said.

The lady would turn back and look at the Chief's Brother.

"You are what they call a shaman, are you not?" She said.

"Yes, that is right. So, who are you?" He asked.

"I am the one known as Sek-Met, wife of Anubis, and this cat is my sister's avatar. I came to pay my respects and uphold my promise to Morgan."

Chief Wahoo's Brother's eyes went wide. He could not believe who was standing in front of him. "You are the Egyptian Cat Goddess?" he asked, surprised.

Sek-Met smiled. "That is correct. Are you saying you did not know what Morgan was doing after leaving the Army?" She asked.

"Jay kept to himself and very seldom came home. Usually, it was only for a day or two, and he would be off." The Shaman said

"I see, well, you see, Morgan was a special hunter, and he wanted a clean slate. He felt he dishonored his ancestors. I gave him away to atone for what he had done. He accepted, and I always kept my word. "Sek-Met told him.

151

"Interesting, so two last questions, if you will permit me?" He asked Sek-Met

"Alright, two questions, and then I must depart," Sek-Met said.

"One, where is my Nephew really at? His spirit, that is." The Shaman asked.

"Morgan is resting with his Ancestors and the Great Spirit. As all Comanche Warriors rest." Sek-Met said.

"Thank you, now my last question. Why did your sister's cat, the Totem go to the Queen and not to one of the Comanche?" He asked.

Sek-Met smiled "This information I will hold you to keep secret. For the Queen is family and my Granddaughter." Sek-Met said.

The Shaman was shocked by what he heard. "The Queen is your ... Granddaughter... your serious ... that would explain things. My Nephew got to work for a Goddess. That is something I will be happy to keep. But may I tell my brother Morgan's father." The Shaman asked.

Sek-Met smiled. "That is acceptable, but only after Mary is on her way back home to her kingdom." She told the Shaman.

The Shaman just nodded and turned to walk away. But then he turned back and found no one, not even the cat, was around. The Shaman went back to the celebration. He would later tell his brother what had happened after Mary had left.

The following day, everyone was up and escorted to the airport. Mary and Albert would meet one last time with Morgan's Family. Chief Wahoo thanked Mary for bringing his son home one last time. Then they walked everyone out to the plane as the Royal Guard waited for Mary and Albert to go on to the plane. Once everyone was on board the plane, Morgan's Family would watch from the tarmac as the aircraft would taxi down to the runway, then turn and go through the checklist before taking off and heading back to Boldovia.

# 25

# Teveahna Rebuilt and Rise of VonStine Castle

Three years had passed since the night of Carmella's attack on the city of Teveahna. But now, all of the destruction that totally destroyed all of the downtown area and even the VonStine Castle and Manor house that once stood upon the mountain was all gone. But in the aftermath, a new city had finally risen to show that the country was back on its feet and the royal family was alive and well.

Where once the VonStine castle and Manor house stood, a new fortress had been built. This fortress was not a castle but more of a military base along with several places around the area where the Manor house once was. This area was the new home for the Lord of the werewolves and the werewolf army that was now the protectors of the city of Teveahna. This was a military compound and fortress with multiple buildings for all the soldiers and their families. This was all a reward for their help in fighting Carmella that night. The Lord of the Werewolves was also one of the Queen's advisors since the wolves could not return to Monico for political reasons. The base was set with a large keep and several smaller houses around this keep, along with a massive tunnel and housing inside the mountain itself.

The city of Teveahna also changed, for most of the town had been destroyed in the fighting. The city square was the first to be rebuilt, and it had changed. The train station was no longer in the heart of the city, for it had been moved to the outskirts of the town on its eastern side to implement a much larger station with six lines coming into the city. It is set just to the west of the crossroads.

Due to all the destruction that had taken place, the Tivoctive River had to be rerouted. So, the river was set using massive concrete barriers to run through the city's heart to make what could be seen as an enormous island in the middle of the town. The island part of the city was lined with a concrete barrier to stop any erosion, and seven bridges were built around it to connect the rest of the town.

On the outer part of the river rose new skyscrapers that went around the main square. These buildings were new condominiums and parking garages, and massive shopping malls set in the towers on different floors to give a more classic feeling to shopping. A total of fifteen buildings were built. With six as residential condominiums, five as shopping malls, one as the new radio and television station, and one as the new hospital and nursing home. The last two buildings were the new City School Board building, and last but not least, the last was a massive domed building that housed the royal library and music hall.

The rest of the not damaged or destroyed city was all checked and updated with all new roads and several new fire stations and schools.

As you moved to the south of the Island arose the new city hall. The city hall was a massive domed building in what looked to be made out of white marble but, in truth, was a white concrete that was made to look like marble. The new City hall housed all City officials and works such as water and so on. On the City Hall's west wing were the new police station and courthouse. On the south side of the central dome were all the records offices. The East side of the courthouse housed all the city officials and a new meeting room. This courthouse was state of the art, and it shined in the sunlight.

Finally, as you went over the bridge to the south, you saw the city's heart. In the heart, from the south going north on each side of the bridge rose six massive skyscrapers, all different but breathtaking in looks. With all six towers, the parking area was hidden below them, and the entrance was near the back of each building, so you could not drive into the city's heart. The road circled behind all the buildings on each side up to the last building.

In the heart of the center was a massive statue fountain display. The display was of the Great Prince along with Mary's Father Victor, posed like the old one but much more prominent. There were four more monuments to the north, south, east, and west of the central fountain.

The one to the north was of Jay Lester Morgan, the Queen's first knight who had fallen in the battle. It depicted Morgan standing tall in ceremonial armor with the Queen's banner. A fitting monument to a man who sacrificed himself to save so many.

The monument to the east was of the pack members who had died on the night of the VH attack, and it showed them all standing in ceremonial armor with each coat of arms the Queen awarded them.

The monument to the west was that of soldiers standing in their World War II uniforms and a plaque with all those who had fallen in the war's names listed.

The monument to the south was of the Count Valdisoph Vicious VonKomfoang and the Great Prince Nicolas VonStine on horses in their knight armor as if defending the city and honoring them for their sacrifice.

At the north end of the Island arose the new VonStine castle. This castle was massive. In fact, it housed three separate keeps. The keep that sat north was the main keep this housed the Queen and her family. It was much larger than the old one with three main floors. Unlike the two the old one housed. It shined in the sun as it was all white with the roof a bright blue color. The top floor in the castle was the privet chamber of the Queen and her husband. On this floor was a Master bedroom, two side bedrooms, a private office, a massive bathroom for the Master bedroom, and one hall bathroom for the other two bedrooms. The second floor was family bedrooms and bathrooms, a set of six bedrooms and three bathrooms on the floor. The first floor housed a massive kitchen like the old keep and royal office. But the throne room now sat in the middle of the castle on this floor, and between it and the kitchen was the hallway with an elevator located to access the other floors.

The throne room was like the one Mary had seen in England. It was all red with beautiful red trimmed in gold carpet, and two thrones sat on the raised area. To each side were two different rooms, one a room all in blue and copied the blue drawing-room from England.

The room to the west side was the massive dining hall. To the south of all this was the entry off-center for protection reasons. A hallway led to the garage area where the royal cars were kept to the west end of the entry. The Integra was gone, for it was destroyed along with the Rolls Royce. Now sitting in the garage as a new Rolls Royce and a new Auston Martin DB11.

Another walkway led to the keep on the east side which was located just to the east side of the entry. This keep was a copy of the original one that once was on the mountain and is now home to Count Valdisoph Vicious VonKomfoang and his wife, Mina.

As you came out of the keep on the east side, you found a lovely fountain and flagstaff with two flags flying, One was the flag of the country of Boldovia, and the other was the Royal Flag of the VonStines.

Past the fountains to the west set the third keep just like the keep on the east side, but this was the home of Baron VonStine and his wife, the lady Lillian Diana VonStine. And around all three of the keeps was a massive wall that had battlements at every fifty feet and an enormous gatehouse at the south end that opened out to the square.

Just to the east of the new castle was the new St. John's Cathedral, and it looked just like the old one that had been destroyed in all its glory.

At the front were new statues of Christ and the Disciples. New massive doors with all new carvings sat at the entrance. As you came inside the Auditorium was set as a cross with high vaulted ceilings along with new stained glass windows that the sun shined through. At the cross intersection to the left was the sitting area of the royal family. To the right was the Piano and at the front was the stage where the Bishop stood and behind him was the Chorial area for the Choir.

Behind the Choir area was another massive stained glass window with a cross in it.

The whole city shined in all its beauty as more and more people came in. The Queen also brought in new casino's into the area drawing on Monico on how they did things as well. Mary had said she was going to make her country safe and prosperous and after so long she had finally done it.

But today was unique as the Royal Rolls Royce had left the keep and pulled up in front of the Cathedral. The whole family had been there waiting on the Rolls to pull up. As the door opened, Albert was first to get out.

Albert helped Mary out, and with them were their twins, that had been born only two month ago. A Boy named Edward David VonStine, and a Girl named Rebecca Isis VonStine. Today was the day of their christening, and all were there for the moment. Edward was holding his little girl Mary Margret VonStine who had just turned three and at his side was his wife, Tasha VonStine.

"Daddy, are they getting baptized?" Mary Margret asked her father, Edward.

Edward smiled at his daughter. "Yes, Mary, they are getting baptized today just like you did when you were little," Edward explained to his daughter.

Albert and Mary walked into the Cathedral. They were followed by the family and came in for the ceremony. The Bishop and all those inside wished for a peaceful and happy future for the new prince and princess.

# 26

# The Future of Boldovia and its Queen

Finally, peace had come to Boldovia, but the old Capital would never be the same as the world learned the truth about the counties dark secret and past. However, things were not as one would think. The City of Teveahna was now more prominent than ever, and more and more people we coming into the city to learn of the monsters that roamed the country.

The Count these days, along with his lovely wife Mina, would go once a week to the music hall and give a lecher on the country's history and talk about his life and how the family survived all these years. The Count seemed to enjoy this lifestyle now. He did not need to hide or worry about what the world thought of him and the VonStine family.

On a crystal clear night, the train from the Capital pulled in. The train's attendance took care to secure it as it came to a stop at the station. Inside the last car sat a man with short black hair and a trim mustache. He was dressed in a casual suit and tie with a gold tipped cane resting at his side. Across from him was a pale red haired woman who seemed to be in her early thirties. She was in a lovely light blue dress that hugged her body, and her hair laid softly on her shoulders.

As The man stood up, one of the train's conductors entered the car.

"Sir, we are at the last stop. I hope you enjoyed the trip to Teveahna," He told the couple.

The man looked to the train conductor and nodded slightly. "Yes, we did. Thank you," He replied as the lady with red hair took his hand and stood up. The train conductor showed the couple to the exit.

The couple stepped off the train and looked around at the new train station.

"My, what a remarkable looking train station. This must have cost a fortune to build." The lady with red hair said.

"Yes, Crystal, it must have, but if I recall, Edward had a massive treasure when he died. If that is still around then, the Queen should still have a large fortune even after doing all this. "The man told the red haired lady.

Crystal took the arm of the dark haired man as they walked down the street, heading to the city's heart. They were enjoying the night. It was clear, and the moon shined on the city. The lights were set like they were in the late eighteen hundreds and made the city feel old. But in truth, everything was all new and modern.

People were out at restaurants eating outside, and just enjoying the night. The couple was happy to see all this going on. They heard people talk about the werewolves on the mountain and how the wolves had met with people. They learned about the Count, and his wife, Mina, who were both vampires and had finished a talk at the concert hall on being vampires and their lives over the past five hundred years.

Crystal looked to her companion. "This seems like paradise in a way, my love," She said.

The dark haired man nodded and smiled. "Yes, it does. But remember, we are just visiting." He said.

Crystal smiled as they kept walking. The couple finally made it to the heart of the city, and as they looked around, they went over to each of the statue monuments.

They stopped at the monument of The Great Prince and Victor VonStine, Mary's father.

"So that is Prince Edward; you always talk about love?" Crystal asked the dark haired man.

The dark haired man looked at the statue of Edward closely. "Yes, that is Edward, and it looks just like he did back then. "He told Crystal. But they did not know the other man and had to read the plaque. It stated that the man by Edward was the father of the Queen and served in the United States Army. Which surprised the couple.

"So that is the Queens father interesting, so the Queen is American by birth then. Even more interesting." The man said.

As the couple looked at the statue, a police officer walked by and asked if they were doing alright and needed any help. The dark haired man shook his head and thanked the office. The officer let them be and kept on his patrol.

The couple walked up through the center of town. They finally made it to the front gate of the new VonStine Castle.

"My look at this, what an improvement from the old castle. I do like this," The dark haired man said.

The Royal Guards came out to see what the couple needed.

"Greetings, Is there something we could do for you?" One Guard asked.

"Oh yes, I have a prearranged meeting with Count Valdisoph Vicious VonKomFoang." The dark haired man said.

"What is your name Sir?" The Guard asked.

"I am Prince Vadisloff Von Dracu Tempest, and this is my wife, Crystal. We are expected tonight at eleven." The man stated.

The Guard walked into the Guardhouse to check and see if a Prince Tempest had an appointment. The Guard came back out and bowed to the couple.

"If you follow me, I will escort you to the Count and his wife." The Guard said.

The Prince and his wife followed behind the Guard through the main gates. When they came through the other side, the Prince stopped and looked around, seeing that there were three keeps and not just one main one.

"This is interesting. There are three keeps behind the walls. "The Prince said.

"Yes, Prince, you see, the keeps are set where the Baron and Baroness live in one keep, The Count and Countess live in another, and then the Queen and the Prince live in the large one." The Guard said, not knowing he was under the Prince's control for the moment.

The Prince found all this information interesting as they walked to the minor keep on the east side of the courtyard.

The Guard knocked on the main door. The group waited for a few moments before the door was open. A young lady stood at the door looking at the Guard. "Good evening. Can I help you?" She asked.

"Good evening, Prince Vadisloff Von Dracu Tempest and his wife have a scheduled meeting with the Count." The Guard said.

The lady looked at the two people standing behind the Guard and then back to the Guard. "One moment, please." She said.

The lady went and picked up the phone and contacted Velmar to give him the information. She would wait for a few moments. The lady would hang up the phone and walk back to the door where the Guard was with the couple.

"If you will follow me, please, Prince," she said.

The Count and Mina were enjoying their time in the main hall of their keep, which was part of the new VonStine Castle complex; they were sitting near the fireplace. Velmar entered the main chamber where the Count and Mina were at. "Master, you have visitors," Velmar announced.

The Count and Mina both looked at Velmar, "oh, and who might that be?" the Count asked.

Velmar replied, "A Prince Vadisloff Von Dracu Tempest and Lady Crystal Tempest of Moldavia. "

The Count stood up and looked to be readying himself for a fight keeping himself in front and to the side of Mina. "Very well, show them in," The Count said, not wanting to be rude or cause a significant incident.

Velmar left the room and would return shortly with the two visitors. As they entered, Velmar said, "Prince Vadisloff Von Tempest, and the lady Crystal Marie Von Tempest. "

The Prince was in a black suit with a black tie and walked with a cane. His hair was cut short with just a tad of grey, making him look in his late forties to early fifties. The lady at his side looked to be around thirty, with long red hair. She was in a stylish blue dress that went with the day's fashions.

The Count knew precisely who he was and what he was. For Prince Tempest was the Vampire who was the master of Carmella, and the Count did not want to have a fight in the keep if one was to break out.

"Welcome, Prince Tempest, and what do I own this pleasure?" The Count asked politely.

The Prince looked at the Count and smiled. He was not trying to hide anything. After all, the two men had known each other for hundreds of years. "Ah, it has been a very long time since last we stood face to face, and I believe this is the first time I have the pleasure of meeting your lovely wife. Her name is Mina if I remember correctly, is it not?' The Prince said politely.

Mina smiled. "That is correct, Prince Tempest," Mina said in a soft toned voice.

The Count was still on Guard and never let his eyes wander off the Prince. "I came to ask only one question, my dear Count. Exactly what happened to my dear wife, Carmella?" The Prince said with a polite voice that seemed out of the ordinary to the Count.

The Count replied. "Carmella started a war and lost and was judged accordingly." The Count kept between the Prince and Mina just in case the Prince was going to try something.

The Prince did look upset and asked in an agitated voice," Who had the right to Judge Carmella?"

Before the Count could answer, a door on the north side of the room opened, and none other than the Queen Mary Jade VonStine walked in. "Oh, I hope I am not interrupting anything, grandfather," Mary said.

The Prince was surprised to see someone as beautiful as Mary walk in. The Prince looked at the Count. "Grandfather?" he asked, questioning.

"I prefer to call him that since he is family, and I hate calling him count. "Mary said politely.

The Count was shocked to see Mary up and around at this time of night. But here she was, joining everyone.

"Ah this is Prince Vadisloff Von Dracu Tempest of Moldavia. Prince Tempest, this is her Royal Highness Queen Mary Jade VonStine." The Count Stated.

Mary was in jeans and a sweater, not expecting anyone would be visiting this late at night. "Greetings, Prince Tempest. Please excuse my clothing. I was not expecting anyone to visit this late at night. Might I ask what brought you to visit so late at night?" Mary asked.

The Count keep moving some to keep Mary and Mina safe. Velmar noticed what the Count was doing and was also ready just in case but kept in an area to seem non-aggressive.

The Prince looked at Mary and smiled. "I came to ask your so-called Grandfather what happened to my wife, Carmella Valmor." The Prince said to Mary. The Prince's voice was still somewhat agitated.

Mary's smile went away as she looked at the Prince. "Your wife declared war on my family and my country, and she lost, and I judged her in the end. "Mary said with a more authoritative voice.

The Prince, still looking at Mary, smiling but not a happy smile; he showed what he was. But to his surprise, Mary was not affected by him. "And what was your judgment to my wife?" The Prince asked in a somewhat angry voice.

"I gave her peace and let her rest for all time along with her son. She had suffered enough, and I felt she did not need to suffer anymore." Mary said in a soft-toned voice.

The Prince was shocked by what Mary said, "Wait, you did not seek retribution for all Carmella did or torture and pain. You did none of those things. Just let her die in peace and rest in peace with her son for all times," The Prince said, still in some shock, and his voice showed it.

Mary smiled. "I am a just queen, and I rule as a just queen. My personal feelings do not play into my rulings, no matter how much I want them to. I must go by what the laws allow and what is right." Mary said to the Prince.

The Prince looked at Mary for a moment and then at the Count and Mina. "I apologize for all the pain my wife brought upon your family," the Prince stated and then looked back at Mary. "You are a fascinating queen. I will give you that, my dear. But one day we will meet again. Unlike Carmella, I am a patient man, and I have all the time in the world. We will not keep you any longer. Good evening and may we meet like this again on friendly terms. "The Prince said.

Mary smiled "perhaps one day Prince Tempest. Perhaps one day we will. Enjoy your evening," Mary said as Velmar walked the Prince and his wife out of the keep.

Mary looked at the Count and Mina. "Well, that was interesting. You will have to tell me about him someday." Mary said.

The Count smiled. "One day I will, I promise, and how are Albert and the twins doing this night. "The Count said.

Mary, The Count, and Mina went out of the main hall and to the Count's study to relax and talk. As Prince Dracu Tempest and his Bride Crystal walked the night streets enjoying the evening it was all new to them that people mostly now did not fear them. The Prince started to think about things and looked up at the moon and smiled.

"Ah the future is so bright. I have not felt this alive in ages" The Prince said and walked off with his bride into the night.

# The End ?

Dracula created by Bram Stoker

Thank you from the bottom of my heart

James D Lee

Printed in the USA
CPSIA information can be obtained
at www.ICGtesting.com
JSHW011608310824
68977JS00012B/171

9 798885 907217